The Real Housewives

of

Adverse City 4

SCANLIFE

Get more Info About Shelia E. Bell books!

HIS PEN
PUBLISHING LLC

More Perfect Stories About Imperfect People by Shelia E. Bell
(Some titles remain under former name Shelia Lipsey)

Young Adult Titles
House of Cars
The Life of Payne
The Lollipop Girl
The Righteous Brothers (Coming 2019)

Standalone Novels
Show A Little Love (*out of print*)
Always Now and Forever Love Hurts
Into Each Life
Sinsatiable
What's Blood Got To Do With It?
Only In My Dreams
The House Husband
Cross Road
Forever Ain't Enough

Series Books

Beautiful Ugly
True Beauty (*sequel to Beautiful Ugly*)

My Son's Wife Series
My Son's Wife: The Beginning (Book 1)
My Son's Ex-Wife: Aftershock (Book 2)
My Son's Next Wife (Book 3)
My Sister My Momma My Wife (Book 4)
My Wife My Baby...And Him (Book 5)
The McCoy's of Holy Rock (Book 6)
Dem McCoy Boys (Book 7)
My Brother, Father...And Me (Book 8)
My Truth, My Time, My Turn (Book 9)

What Readers Are Saying

Flawless Plot
"I met this author in Memphis a few years ago and was truly impressed with her work. Once I dove into the lives of the housewives. I was freaking hook. She designs every character to leave a permanent stain on your brain. This book was better than watching any reality show on TV. Author Shelia Bell always starts her work off with a fascinating quote to jump start the chapter. These ladies are rich, famous, and scandalous. Each one has secrets and their husbands are no better. From the church to the closets. This book will have you gasping for breath with every page turn. It's a good thing I was behind because I order the sequel as soon as I finish the first one. Love it!" Flenardo

"This book was drama from beginning to end. I don't usually read or watch anything regarding Housewives, but this peaked my interest. Meesha, Peyton, Avery, and Eva had a lot of secrets . Can't wait to read next book." Ms. A.

"I'm truly blessed to have known Shelia Bell for so many years. Your books have been an inspiration to me and my daughter A'kymara and my family throughout the years! We love you dearly, Miss Shelia. You are God's blessed girl." Carolyn Denise Rooks

DRAMA, DRAMA and more DRAMA! "I really enjoyed reading this page turner. Shelia Bell has penned another great read. I love following the characters in this book to see what they are up to next. I must say that Carlton is a trip. I found myself experiencing many emotions and talking to the characters in this book and sometimes just shaking my head. If you are looking for a good read check out this series. I recommend starting from Book 1." The Book Diva

The Real Housewives

of

Adverse City 4

Get more Info About Shelia E. Bell books!

SHELIA E. BELL

ISBN-13: 978-1-944643-21-8

Printed in the United States of America

Library of Congress Control Number: 2019902577

Acknowledgements

"Friendship is the hardest thing in the world to explain. It's not something you learn in school. But if you haven't learned the meaning of friendship, you really haven't learned anything." Muhammad Ali

I acknowledge and thank all of my 'friends'. That includes my family, especially my sons, grandchildren, and siblings. To those who I can honestly call *authentic friends*. You know the kind of people who love you when you are not so lovely. The kind of people who help you face the adversities of this sometimes difficult life. The one who sees you at your worst but still manage to bring out your best. I want to tell you while there is breath in my lungs and the blood runs warm in my veins—I love you. I thank God for you. I thank God for being the best friend a woman like me could ever have. He's the one who knows *all* of my secrets. Those things about me that even I am sometimes ashamed to think about. Yet, He has never ever turned his back on me. For that I am so grateful, God.

Shelia E. Bell
God's Amazing Girl

1

"Silly me. Expecting too much from people again." Unknown

"Noooo, stop. Oh, God. *Please. Pleeease,* Harper." Eva threw up both hands to cover her face to shield herself from Harper's blows. Only he wasn't hitting her in the face—that would leave visible bruises and marks. He'd learned better. He hit her across her shoulders, her back, and her breasts.

"When will you learn? There's nothing you can do, no where you can go that I won't find out. You're so stupid! I'll find out every time what you're doing behind my back."

Eva helplessly tried to tear herself away from Harper but her petite, 105 pound frame was no match against the towering Harper.

Knock. Knock.

"Is everything okay?" Marissa asked from the other side of her employer's closed bedroom door.

Eva would not admit to Marissa that Harper was beating her. Marissa didn't need a verbal confession. She'd seen the bruises on Senora

Eva for the past several months—heard the beatings that often took place late at night or before the rising of the sun. Senora Eva's personality was different as well. She used to be so bubbly, happy, and just an all-around sweet lady. All that had changed. Eva was distant, timid acting, almost behaving like a frightened animal.

It wasn't quite noon. Marissa ventured upstairs to Eva and Harper's side of the spacious mansion to make sure the weekly housekeeping crew had done the things Dr. Stenberg had specifically asked them to do.

Housekeeping wasn't officially part of Marissa's job description. She was the Stenberg's private, full-time chef. But she was responsible for any and all hired help that came and went in and out of the Stenberg residence.

Marissa didn't want to get in trouble, but she couldn't pass by their bedroom and pretend like she didn't hear Eva's screams and Dr. Stenberg's vile stream of verbal attacks.

She knocked on the door again and repeated the question. "Senor Harper, is everything okay? Senora Eva?"

Harper halted his attack when he heard Marissa's voice and turned toward the door.

"Everything's good, Marissa. Please, leave us alone."

"Yes, everything is fine. Go downstairs, Marissa. I'll be down there shortly," Eva said immediately after fighting back tears. *Thank God for Marissa.*

Eva took the opportunity to escape to their bathroom. She turned on the water and began to wash her face in cold water.

Harper followed. "Why do you make me do this? Why can't you be like the woman I married? The woman I fell in love with? You thought I wouldn't find out about you working at that Godforsaken dog place! I can't believe my wife would embarrass me by going behind my back, groveling to someone else like you need handouts or something."

Eva turned off the cold wáter and looked at Harper, still whimpering. "I've done nothing wrong. How many times have you told me to get a hobby, find something to do with my time, go to school, get involved in this, do that? What's wrong with you, Harper? How could you treat me this way?"

"That didn't mean go get a job behind my back, and of all places for you to," he threw up his hands still angry, "work or volunteer as you put it. Whatever you call yourself doing you're

3

doing it for Quentin Winters? You're talking about me? How could you?"

He grabbed hold of her elbow, turned her towards him, and pulled her into his chest. Rubbing her hair, he then kissed her on top of her head.

"Why do you do this to me? You drive me insane with jealousy. I can't stand the thought of another man touching you, Eva. I've tried to forgive you for sleeping with my son, my one and only son at that, but every time I think I can, you do something like this. You go behind my back."

Eva eased away from him, being extra careful not to anger him again by moving from his grasp suddenly. At this point she had begun to hate Harper. A man she once loved and adored.

"I didn't go behind your back. I just didn't tell you because I knew you would react like this. I love animals. You know that, Harper. It's the only reason I accepted his offer to volunteer at his rescue shop."

At the same time, as if they could read her mind, her three pups started barking from outside the door.

"I don't know how you call yourself loving animals when you don't even take care of the ones you have," Harper barked. "Anyway, as of today, you're no longer a volunteer at Quentin Winston's mutt shelter. Do you understand me?"

"Why are you doing this? You're gone all the time. You have your books, your TV show, your work at Adverse City General and you want me to do what?"

"I want you to do what I tell you to do. I want you to be the wife I need you to be. That's what I want."

He turned around, left the bathroom, and then opened the bedroom door. The dogs ran inside, causing him to trip. He mouthed an expletive and then stormed out of the room.

Eva finished cleaning herself up and then went back and sat down on top of the cold white toilet. So this is what my life has resulted to," she cried. "I might as well be a prisoner. I wonder if he's even going to let me finish my last few weeks of culinary school. God, I need you to help me."

Marissa appeared moments later. "Senora." She knelt down beside the toilet while the dogs yelped at both of their feet. "Go," Marissa ordered the dogs and they scurried off. She took hold of Eva's hand, almost crying when she saw Eva's bruised face.

Eva stood up. Marissa copied. "Please let me see."

Eva, for the first time, obeyed Marissa, unbuttoned her blouse, and let it fall off her shoulders.

Marissa gasped when she saw the deep dark purple bruises on Eva's chest, her small breasts, her belly, and her back.

"You need doctor."

"No!" Eva yelled and then immediately regretted the tone she took with Marissa. Marissa had nothing but Eva's best interest at heart. "No, please, no doctors, Marissa. I'll be okay. I promise. Where is he? Did he leave?"

"Yes, he left for the TV studio and then he said he will be at hospital until late this evening."

Eva exhaled, walked out of the bathroom, and then went over to the chair in her bedroom and sat down.

"Would you like me to make you some hot turmeric tea? It will help you feel better?"

Eva nodded. "That sounds good."

Marissa turned to leave out of the bedroom but stopped at the door. "I'll fix you something to eat, too. Si?"

"*Si, gracias*, Marissa." She watched as Marissa walked out of the room, closing the door behind her.

Eva's cell phone rang. Already getting sore and stiff, she managed to reach over to the side of the chair and pick up the phone from the night table.

"Ugghh," she moaned in pain as she looked at her phone. It said CULINARY SHOP, which meant it was Quentin calling. She knew better than to list his name in her CONTACTS. She touched the ANSWER button. "Hello." Eva tried to sound as normal as possible.

"Where are you? You were supposed to be here two hours ago. Did you forget we had that rescue this morning? You know the call about the abused dogs that came in through the answering service."

Eva shook her head and placed a hand on her forehead. She'd forgotten all about the call. Harper's beating had taken precedence over her plans and it left her mind that she'd promised Quentin she would go with him on the rescue mission. Little did he know, she needed her own rescuing.

"Um, I'm sorry. Yes, I uh, I forgot all about it."

Quentin listened. Something was off. It wasn't like Eva to forget about an animal rescue. She was the one who often had to remind him of what was going on at the shelter. "Are you all right?"

Eva sucked in a silent breath and then exhaled before answering. "Sure, I'm fine. It's just that, well Harper wants me to spend more time helping him with promoting his books and working behind the scenes on *Heart of the Matter*. The TV show is a huge hit and well, he thought I could start being part of the show, you know prepare dishes live on TV once a week." What she said wasn't exactly a lie. Harper had mentioned her joining him on the TV show as a heart healthy chef. In the past she would have jumped at such an opportunity, but she knew Harper only wanted her to be part of the show as another way to keep track of her.

"That sounds good, but does this mean you're no longer going to be my assistant director? I need you, Eva. I've come to rely on you."

His voice was sincere, masculine, sexy. Eva loved every moment she spent next to Quentin Winters. He made her forget about what she often faced when Harper was in town and on one of his rampages.

"I wish I could do both, but I can't."

Marissa appeared in the doorway with a tray of food and tea.

"Look, I have to go, Quentin. We'll talk later. I'm sorry." Abruptly, Eva ended the call.

2

"Don't walk behind me; I may not lead. Don't walk in front of me; I may not follow. Just walk beside me and be my friend." Albert Camus

Peyton felt free as she cruised up Adverse City Boulevard singing along with the tune playing on the radio. This was her first time behind the wheel of a car since the accident almost two years ago. She usually had a private chauffeur take her wherever she wanted to go. No more. Her license and driving privileges had been restored, she was off probation, had paid her fines, and she felt good.

The accident almost destroyed her life, her marriage, her relationship with her son, all because of the irrational decision she made to get behind the wheel drunk and angry. She could have killed the two police officers she rammed with her Maybach C600. Thank God, she was able to make an out of court settlement with the officers, attend a virtual alcohol class from home, and do probation. All of that was in the past now. She didn't care what others thought; money *does* answer some prayers—it certainly answered hers.

Her happy spirit was thrown for a loop when she stopped at the traffic light. Looking in her rearview mirror, she saw a couple behind her. They were obviously having some kind of disagreement. She gasped in horror when she recognized Eva sitting on the passenger side and Harper in the driver's seat. When she saw him backhand Eva, Peyton's hand automatically went up and over her mouth. Without thinking, she put her hand on the door handle and was about to get out of her car but thank God the light changed, bringing her back to reality. Sitting there, she didn't move until she heard Harper's, or what she assumed was Harper's horn going off, signaling her to get to moving.

Still trying to look through her mirror as she drove off, she lost sight of them when he turned right on the next street. "That wasn't them. Probably just a couple who looked like them," she mouthed. Who was she fooling? It was them all right. But seeing Harper backhand slap Eva like she was a rag doll was totally out of character for the accomplished doctor, author, and TV host—wasn't it?

Her cell phone started ringing inside the spank brand new diamond white Mercedes

Maybach S650 Sedan. She glanced at the dash, and her mind came back to the mission at hand. *That wasn't Eva and Harper,* she told herself again and shrugged it off.

"Hi, I'm almost there."

"Okay, I was just checking to see if you'd left home yet."

"Yes, I ate breakfast with Liam before he left for school. Then I had to get ready. I should be there in about ten or fifteen minutes. I'm so glad you agreed to go with me to the fertility specialist."

"I'm glad I could do it. That's the perks of being the administrator of Perfecting Your Faith Academy and having your husband as Senior Pastor. I can come and go as I please." Meesha laughed.

"Yea, you got that right, but I know how much you love that school and the role you serve. For you to be willing to go with me instead of going to work today, well, it means everything to me."

Meesha waved her hand in the air as she talked to Peyton. "Girl, that's what friends are for. As for the Academy, Kingston is the best assistant headmaster any school could ask for. I don't have to worry about a thing."

"I guess that's another perk, huh? Having your husband's brothers working in the church and at the Academy."

"Yea, I guess so," Meesha agreed and laughed as she held Makena Grace in her arms.

"I'll see you soon."

"Okay, bye." Meesha ended the call and focused on her little girl. She gave her slobbery kisses. "I love you, Makena. Mommy loves you *soooo* much."

"What about me? Does Mommy love me too?" Carlton strolled into the family room and walked up to his wife and baby girl.

"Of course we do, don't we Makena?" She leaned in and meshed Carlton's lips with hers. The two of them engaged in a long, lingering kiss.

When he pulled back, he looked down at Makena who was looking curiously at both of her parents with a weird but cute expression on her ten month old cherub face.

Carlton scooped his daughter out of his wife's arms and kissed the little girl on her forehead then raised her up and down in the air. Makena released loud giggles, indicating her approval.

Meesha stood up, folded her arms, and smiled. She loved seeing Carlton with Makena.

He was so good with her, the same as he was when the boys were babies like her. He still remained an involved father to their four boys, something Meesha felt truly blessed by.

"What's your schedule like today?" Makena grabbed at her father's bottom lip and tugged on it while he talked.

"Peyton asked me if I would go with her to her doctor's appointment." Meesha wasn't going to divulge to Carlton the kind of doctor Peyton was going to see. She promised she would keep that confidential until Peyton decided otherwise. So far, only the other housewives knew about her plans to get pregnant. She hadn't even discussed it with Derek yet. Peyton said she wanted to keep it mum until the fertility specialist told her the chances she had of getting pregnant.

"You aren't taking Makena with you, are you?"

"No, she's going to stay here. I might stop by PYF when I leave Peyton, that is depending on how long her doctor's appointment lasts."

"Why would you do that? I mean, Kingston can handle whatever comes up at the academy. I told you, Meesha, you don't have to be at the academy every single day. You're the administrator, sure, but you have a great staff and the school almost runs itself now. You're

13

busy enough with the kids, especially Makena."

"Yes, I know, sweetheart, but I have an obligation to Perfecting Your Faith and that includes the academy. It's my heart. You named me the administrator when God gave you the vision to start the school. It's been a blessing to me. I don't want to take it for granted."

Carlton kissed her lightly again on her lips. "You're taking nothing for granted. You're First Lady and that in and of itself requires a lot of you. I don't want you to feel like your life and all of your free time has to be spent at Perfecting Your Faith or at the academy. Enjoy your life outside of those walls, these walls." He looked around, extended his arm out, and scanned the room with his eyes, holding Makena with the other hand.

"Thanks, Carlton. I promise you I'll spend more time doing nothing." She smiled again.

Carlton chuckled the same time his phone chimed. "Well, that's my cue. I'm heading to Perfecting Your Faith now. I'll try to be home in time for dinner."

"See, you're the one who spends almost every waking hour at that church. Not that I'm complaining, I'm just saying."

"You got me, but nothing is going to come between my beautiful wife and my family. You got that?"

"I got that."

Meesha and Carlton kissed again. He passed Makena to her mommy and the couple said their goodbyes before Meesha went to seek the nanny to pass off Makena to her.

Ω

"I'm so excited, Meesha. What if I'm able to give Derek a kid?" Peyton was overcome with joy. She grabbed hold of Meesha's hand and squeezed it as they exited the doctor's office and headed to the car.

"Yes, wouldn't that be a blessing. When are you going to talk to Derek about it?" They walked outside and were greeted by the bright sun and perfect Adverse City, Florida weather.

"I think I'm going to make it a special occasion. You know, have the chef prepare Derek's favorite meal and dessert, and then while we're eating I'll bring it up and let him know I want to give him a baby. Or I might take him to his favorite spot, YardBird and tell him then. I don't know. Either way, I'm going to wait until the weekend to talk to him. Liam will be gone with the PYF lacrosse team."

15

"Oh, that's right; the team *does* have a match this weekend in Tampa."

"Yes, they're leaving after school Friday. Meesha, girl, to learn Derek and I can try artificial insemination first but if after what did the specialist say—two or three attempts?"

"Yes, if you haven't gotten pregnant after two or three attempts from artificial insemination he said you can try IVF. Or you can do IVF right off the bat. It's your choice. Girl, thank God money is no issue. So many couples are disappointed and left without children because they don't have the money for fertility treatments or adoption."

"Yes, I know. That's such a shame," Peyton quickly agreed, "but getting back to me and Derek. If we do have to result to IVF we can choose two or three retrievals through that multi-cycle program he told us about which makes the chances of me getting pregnant even better."

"Yea, they'll transfer all your good embryos until you and Derek bring home a baby."

"And under that program it includes an unlimited number of frozen embryo transfers. With either insemination or IVF, I could get pregnant right away. Oh, Meesha, wouldn't that be the best?"

Meesha smiled as they arrived at Peyton's car. *God, if it is your will, bless my friend and her husband with a child. You're the God of second chances. Grant Peyton a second chance to make her life and her marriage better.*

"You hear me, Meesha?"

"Oh, I guess I was lost in my thoughts. What did you say?"

"I said, do you want to stop and get something to eat? I'm famished."

"Yes, let's do it. I'm hungry too."

3

"Nothing weighs on us so heavily as a secret."
Jean de La Fontaine

"What's up with you and church? For the past few weeks you keep coming up with some lame excuse not to go."

"I don't know what you want me to say, Ryker. I've heard the word preached over and over and frankly, I need a rest from the mundane services at Perfecting Your Faith. If I need a word I can watch one of those televangelists. Anyway, my what you call *lame excuse* is I need a break," she said sarcastically.

"I don't like going to church Sunday after Sunday alone. People are asking about you, wondering where you are. Even the girls don't like to go when you don't go."

"Well, the girls don't have a choice. They're going whether they want to or not. When they get of age they can make the decision as to how much they want to be involved. As for the people at church, they're just being nosy. They don't care about me. Fake folks."

"You lead by example, Avery. That's all I'm saying, baby."

"I know, and it's not like I'm never going to go back to Perfecting Your Faith. I said I just need a break."

Ryker showed one palm as he walked over from the kitchen sink to the oversized marble top island where he'd put his sandwich and salad." He placed the cup of coffee he had in his hand next to his plate of food then took a seat in one of the high back bar stools.

Avery couldn't stop thinking about her previous encounter with Carlton. The way he attacked her while she had little RJ was one of the most frightening things she'd ever experienced. What if he had caused her to drop her baby? Oh, God what had he been thinking? More importantly, what had *she* been thinking? How could she ever have gotten mixed up with him in the first place? Thank God little RJ was not his child. She had been so blind to believe there could ever be anything between her and Carlton. *Poor Meesha. She has no idea who she's married to.* And knowing Carlton Porter, he was probably messing around with some other naïve, vulnerable female. Avery wouldn't be surprised, not in the least.

19

"So, what you're saying is you're not going again?"

Avery looked up at Ryker from where she sat on the wraparound sofa. Rolling her eyes, she spoke, "Uh, one more time, NO, I am not going to church *again* today, Ryker. And read my lips—I don't know when I'm going back."

Avery got up with arms folded, walked past her husband, and disappeared out of the room, leaving Ryker stunned. Something was going on. Had Avery had a fight with Meesha or the other housewives? He shook his head, touched his hand against his forehead, and then walked out of the family room.

"Please get RJ," Avery yelled when she heard the little boy crying in his nursery from the sitting room, adjacent to her and Carlton's bedroom. "Somebody," she cried out, "get him."

Avery saw the nanny scurry past the sitting room headed toward the nursery. Lexie trailed immediately after her. Avery watched from the bedroom monitor on her nightstand as the nanny entered RJ's room talking baby talk to him in an effort to get him to stop crying. He'd just woke up from a nap and was cranky and probably had a wet diaper. Lexie spoke soft kind words to her baby brother too as she planted herself next to the nanny.

RJ continued to keep up a fuss as Lexie walked away from his crib and returned a few seconds later with wipes and a pamper that she gave to the nanny.

After he was changed, the nanny picked him up and gave him to his big sister. Lexie loved holding and spoiling her little brother, treating him like one of her baby dolls.

Avery smiled as she watched the chubby little boy start giggling instead of crying. Lexie was a pre-teen now but she still loved to play with her baby dolls and Barbie dolls. She walked with him out of the room and Avery laid back against her bed as the nanny and Lexie disappeared from the monitor.

They walked back past the sitting room, not bothering to stop, which was fine by Avery. She wasn't in the mood to cuddle her little boy. She loved him but her mind was still dealing with the what ifs that could have happened had things gone the way they could have the day she paid that visit to the devil himself—Carlton Porter.

A couple hours later Ryker entered the bedroom and Avery was propped in the bed watching T. D. Jakes of the Potter's House.

"We're about ready to leave for church," he said. "Sure I can't get you to change your mind?"

"No, I'm good. Just be patient with me. Okay?"

Ryker walked over to the bed, leaned down and kissed his wife on her lips. "Sure."

"And if those nosy church folk ask about me please tell 'em to mind their own business."

"You know I wouldn't say any such thing, Avery. I'll tell them you're doing fine. You just need a break."

"Okay, suit yourself, but I wouldn't tell 'em a darn thing. Anyway, y'all have a good time. I'll see you in a couple of hours."

Ryker straightened himself up and smiled.

"You look so handsome," she said as he prepared to turn and leave out of the room.

"Thanks. You like this suit? It's new. I picked it up from the tailor's yesterday."

"Yes. You look like you're worth a million bucks," she said and laughed.

Ryker returned the gesture with a smile of his own. "I'll see you later this afternoon. I'll call you if we decide to stop and get something to eat after church."

"Sounds good. Bye, sweetheart."

With the house quiet, Avery channel surfed as she soaked in the solitude. Her marriage was intact, her girls were growing up, and her son was the icing on the cake. RJ had no idea how he had practically saved the day. God had come through and saved her life yet again. Had RJ turned out to be Carlton's kid, she would be going through pure unadulterated hell right about now.

Ryker expected her to return to Perfecting Your Faith but she would have to pray on that one for a minute. She was still afraid of Carlton and bringing out the side of him she was privy to was something she didn't want to do—ever again.

4

*"You have heard it said, 'Do not commit
adultery'. But I tell you that anyone who looks
at a woman lustfully has already committed
adultery with her in his heart."*
Matthew 5:27, Bible

Meesha tapped with her knuckles and
without waiting on a response, turned the
doorknob and walked into Carlton's office with
Makena Grace in her arms.

"Oh, hey, Evelyn," she said when she saw
her husband's sister-in-law seated in his office.

Evelyn swiveled around in her chair to face
Meesha, smiling. "Hey, girl." Rising from her
chair, she stood and reached for Makena
Grace. "Come here, you pretty little thang."

Makena obliged and leaned her little body
toward Evelyn.

"I didn't mean to interrupt. I didn't know
you were in a meeting."

Carlton shook his head. "Noooo. It's not an
official meeting. Evelyn just stopped by after
service to follow up with me on some things
taking place with the Pastoral Care Ministry."

"Yes, like his birthday is coming up in a few months. I was asking him to start thinking about what he'd like the church as a whole to do. We need to do something to celebrate and show our appreciation for him."

"You know my husband, Evelyn. He's not for all of the hoopla. He likes things to be low key. Every year since he founded Perfecting Your Faith, he's refused to let me acknowledge his birthday in conjunction with something at church."

"Well, now that I'm over the Pastoral Care Ministry I want to see about changing some of his antiquated thinking." Evelyn looked over her shoulder and without Meesha seeing, puckered her lips and smiled at her secret lover.

"If you can do it, then I'll have to definitely give you your props. This man is stubborn as a mule and set in his ways." Meesha laughed.

Evelyn returned her attention to Meesha while kissing Makena Grace on her chubby cheeks. "I'm going to try. He deserves to be celebrated for the man of God he is."

"Okay, enough, ladies. Evelyn, thanks for stopping by. Why don't we get together this week and talk about some of these ideas you have for the Pastoral Care Ministry."

"Sure thing. I'll get on your calendar."

25

Meesha reached for Makena who willingly went back into her mother's arms. "Evelyn, you know you're welcome to come by the house anytime. We're family so don't think the only place and time you can talk to Carlton or me for that matter is at church."

"Thanks, Meesha. You're such a sweetheart." Evelyn walked toward the door, being careful to put an extra switch in her step so Carlton could get a good view of what she was working with. It had been awhile since they'd been together. The last time being when Martin took a group of youth on a weekend trip. She and Carlton had the best time ever in Miami at the Hilton Hotel. They may not have been able to sneak away often because Evelyn had kids too, but when they did hook up they made the best of it without the guilty feelings that often invaded the minds of cheating spouses. Not Carlton and not Evelyn.

Evelyn adored Martin, Carlton's brother, but when it came to satisfying her sexual needs he was lacking. In the bedroom he reminded her of a stuck up, conservative, preacher boy who had been taught to be a gentleman in the bedroom. Being a gentleman in the streets among peers and sophisticated folks was all well and fine. But when they were behind closed doors Evelyn wanted what most men wanted: a freak between the sheets.

From what Carlton had shared with her, Meesha was an identical match to Martin. They were prudes in the bedroom. However, more than Martin, Meesha tried to satisfy Carlton as much as she could but some things she just refused to partake in. Whenever Meesha refused to do certain things in the bedroom, Carlton would spout Hebrews thirteen verse four: *Let marriage be held in honor among all, and let the marriage bed be undefiled.* Meesha would turn right back around and use the same scripture on him but a different translation: *Marriage should be honored by all, and the marriage bed kept pure.*

Carlton being the man he was thought it better not to cause unnecessary discord at home and in his bed. Thus, he satisfied his carnal needs in the arms of other women. Thank God Evelyn Porter understood him.

"How do you think Evelyn is going to do as the director of Pastoral Care?"

"I think it's a perfect fit for her. Like she said, I...we...need someone who will look out for the well-being of the pastor and the pastor's family."

Carlton got up and walked from behind his desk, reaching out for his daughter. "Where are the boys?"

"They should be at home by now."

"Why didn't Yulisa take Makena with them?"

"She offered but I told her no. Mommy couldn't stand to be apart from this little cutie," Meesha cooed, lightly reaching over and pinching Makena's cheek.

"Thank God the boys aren't jealous of their little sister."

"Yes, they're so good with her."

"So do you want to go have a late lunch somewhere before we head home?" Meesha suggested.

"That would be nice, but it'll be a while before I can leave."

He played with Makena while he continued to make up an excuse as to why he couldn't accompany his wife to lunch. All he wanted was to hook up with Evelyn as fast as he could. Martin was taking a group of youth boys to a basketball tournament. That would give him and Evelyn at least three hours of uninterrupted pleasure because he always took his kids along with him whenever he could. That was the reason Evelyn was in his office. They made reservations at their favorite spot—Miami Hilton.

"Awww. Why? What's going on. It's Sunday afternoon. You should be done after preaching at both services."

"Yeah, I know, but a couple of the deacons and trustees are going to a Gators' game. They asked if I'd like to go. You don't mind do you?"

"No, of course not. I mean, you deserve some man time. You hardly ever spend anytime hanging with the boys. Go ahead. I'll head on home."

She reached for Makena Grace and the little girl willfully went back into her mother's arms. "But aren't you going to come home and change?"

"No need. I'll take a quick shower here. You know I keep a wardrobe here so I have a few things I can choose from. Something casual, you know."

"Okay, well tell your daddy buh-bye, Makena." Meesha picked up her baby girl's hand and moved it up and down.

Carlton kissed his little princess and then kissed Meesha, imagining it was Evelyn. His kiss grew so deep and became so heated Meesha stepped back and looked at him with wild abandonment.

"Carlton Porter, don't you start nothing up in Perfecting Your Faith."

Carlton gave her a devious smile. "I can't help it. You have that effect on me."

"I'll see you later this evening, bad boy."

Meesha turned toward the door. Carlton swatted her on her butt as he walked behind her and opened the door for her. "See you later. Bye, my little munchkin," he said to Makena.

As quickly as Meesha stepped on the other side of his office door, Carlton's text notifier pinged. *Ahh, perfect timing.*

"I'm headed there now. You otw?"

"Meesha just left. Give me about 45 minutes. About to leave now."

5

"I love you with all my life, but it's not like you will ever know." Unknown

Quentin was concerned. Days passed and he hadn't seen or heard from Eva. He made a drop in at the culinary school and was told she hadn't been to class in days. That part was unusual too. Eva loved culinary school. She had just weeks before she would graduate. The two of them had talked about him helping her with opening a small restaurant featuring some of her signature Bolivian dishes, which he was glad about.

He tried calling her again but again his call went immediately to her voicemail. The numerous texts he'd sent had gone unanswered as well. Had she blocked his number? If she *had*, why? The only reasonable explanation he could come up with was Harper. He must have discovered Eva was working for him. That was the last thing Eva wanted. She'd made that clear from the very first time they talked about her working at the shelter. He could tell by their conversations the man made Eva uneasy. Whenever Quentin brought his name up, Eva quickly evaded answering any questions or discussing anything about her husband. If he didn't know any better, Quentin might think she was afraid of her own husband. Harper was arrogant, at best, and probably somewhat prideful, but was he so bad that he would keep his wife from doing something she loved and that she was good at?

If she were his he would treat her like a queen. The two of them would work together in his restaurants and with the animals. She would be the perfect mate. But that was neither here nor there. She was already spoken for so he had to make himself content with just having her in his presence as much as possible.

The more Quentin thought about Eva the more uncertain he grew. Had something happened to her? To her family? What could it be? As much as he didn't want to do it, she had left with him no other choice. He had to do what he had to do. Once he found out if she was all right, he would back off. But until then he had to go to the person who would know where she was. Harper.

He got into his car and drove until he arrived at Adverse General Hospital. At first he thought he should go to Eva's house, but like him, she and Harper resided in a private, heavily restricted, gated community.

Arriving at the hospital, he got valet parking, jumped out of his car, and rushed inside. He saw the electronic hospital and physician's directory almost as soon as he entered. Scrolling through the directory, he scanned it until he came to Harper's name. Right away, he jogged through the hospital like he was on a mission and stopped at the first set of elevators. Pushing the UP elevator button, he waited impatiently for the doors to open. When they did, he hurried inside.

A man and woman with two children were on the elevator. "Excuse me." He stepped in front of the man and pushed the button to the 11th floor. The elevator stopped, it seemed, on almost every other floor with people getting on and off, including the family with the kids who got off on the ninth floor.

Ding. The door opened to the 11th floor and Quentin bolted out, stopped, and read the signs before proceeding in the direction of what was to lead to Harper's office.

Approaching the nurses' station he was stopped by one of the nurses seated **behind the counter.**

"Excuse me, sir. How may I help you?" the nurse asked. "There are no patients on this floor. Only on-staff physician offices and the medical director."

"I understand, but I need to see Dr. Stenberg. Is he in his office? Can you tell him Quentin Winters needs to see him."

"I'm sorry, Dr. Stenberg isn't in his office. And he doesn't see walk-ins."

"I'm not a patient. It's a personal matter."

"You can leave a message for him." The name Winters was quite familiar at Adverse General. A whole wing on the cardiology floor was named after the family. The nurse didn't know if this man was part of the Winters' family or somehow who coincidentally bore the same last name. The man didn't say and the nurse didn't ask.

"When do you expect him to return?"

The nurse quickly eyed the nurse sitting next to him. So much was going on these days and the nurse was uneasy about this man who almost demanded to see Dr. Stenberg.

"Dr. Stenberg is out for the remainder of the week."

"Look, I'm sure you've heard of the Winters family. My grandmother, Emma Winters, is one of this hospital's largest donors. And she's a personal and close friend of Dr. Stenberg. I'm her grandson."

"Yes, we're quite familiar with **Mrs. Winters**. And it's nice to meet you, but Dr. Stenberg is not here," the nurse emphasized again, trying his best to remain cordial and not show his mounting aggravation toward this fellow. "Is your grandmother all right? Does she need medical care?"

"No, it's nothing like that. My grandmother is fine. Thank you," Quentin said and turned and dashed off in the direction he'd originally come from.

"Mr. Winters, would you like to leave a message for Dr. Stenberg?"

Quentin flung up one hand without turning back and kept walking down the corridor leading back to the elevator.

"Give Mrs. Winters our regards," the nurse yelled as Quentin disappeared from the hospital corridor.

Ω

Two weeks passed and he still hadn't seen or heard from Eva. He was concerned. He would be out of the country for the next month, at the least, to check on the operations of his restaurant in Paris. He made the trip at least once every two months. His restaurant in

New York was flourishing too and he made a trek there at least two or three times a month. Thank God he had an outstanding executive chef at both restaurants.

If things had worked as he hoped they would, Eva would be in charge of *Scooby Doo's Pet Accessories and Animal Rescue Shelter* during his absence. Unfortunately, that no longer seemed like the case.

He had talked to his grandmother before his scheduled departure and shared his concerns about Eva's sudden unreachability.

"I'll see what I can find out. Harper is out of town but when he returns I'll contact him."

"Yeah, I know. I went to see him at the hospital and I was told he wasn't expected back until next week."

"Why would you do that, Quentin? Eva Stenberg is a married woman. You're Adverse City's most eligible bachelor. I wouldn't be surprised if Harper feels threatened, and I wouldn't blame him. His wife is a beautiful woman. He's an older man and he may have some concerns about his wife hanging around a handsome young man like yourself."

"You're prejudice." Quentin laughed.

"Of course. You're my grandson. I think you and your brother are the cat's meow." Emma Winters broke out in laughter herself.

"I love you, Nana." Quentin and his brother's term of endearment for their grandmother.

"I'm sure everything is all right, sweetheart. The last time Harper and I talked he sounded excited."

"Excited about what?"

"About his wife working with him on his TV show, *The Heart of the Matter*. I'm sure that's why she stopped working with you. I mean, sweetheart, you shouldn't cause unnecessary friction in that marriage."

"What do you mean by that? I'm doing no such thing." Quentin thought about his growing yet unspoken feelings for Eva.

"That girl's first priority should be her husband. If he isn't then she's asking for trouble. Trouble you don't want to be in the middle of."

"Nana, I have no idea what you're talking about."

"Humph, who do you think you're fooling? Certainly not me. I can tell just by looking at you. You're smitten with her. And that's not good, Quentin. I know Harper Stenberg. I've known him for a long time. And let me tell you this, he can be a handful. If I'm aware of that, I'm sure she's aware of it too. So it's best not to ruffle his feathers."

37

Quentin's listening ears perked. What was his grandmother talking about? It sounded like she was saying Harper might have a bit of a temper. That didn't sound good at all.

"Nana, you're talking like dude is a ticking time bomb or something."

"Now, honey, I didn't say that. But let's just say I know some things about Harper I'd rather not talk about. That man literally saved my life. I owe him and I'll remain loyal to him. Of course, wrong is wrong. I wouldn't support him in something that was not right."

"I'm sure you wouldn't but there's nothing between me and Eva. I'm just concerned about her. Wanted to make sure she's good. I mean, she does work for me. Rather, she *did* work for me."

"She told you she couldn't work for you anymore. That's what you told me she said. So leave it alone. Harper is a powerful man and he can be a bit controlling. If he doesn't like what she's doing let that stay between them."

"That's it, Nana; he didn't know about her working for me. She wanted it that way. She wanted to have money of her own, you know. From what she said he didn't give her access to a lot of cash, just his credit cards."

"Again, that's none of your business. Now enough yap about Harper and his wife. Listen to you. I don't care if you deny it or not, it's plain as the nose on your face you're intrigued by this Eva Stenberg woman. All I'm telling you is don't get too close. Find you someone single and free. Messing around with her, you're only asking for trouble."

Quentin kissed and hugged his grandmother. "Thanks, Nana. I love you."

"I love you too. Now scoot. The driver is waiting on you. Call me and do that video thing you young folks do. I want to see your face while you're gone. Maybe you'll bring home one of those French girls and take your mind off Harper's catch."

Quentin kissed and hugged her again. Smiling, he said, "Bye, Nana."

Ω

Quentin sat in the back seat of the onyx black luxury vehicle. His grandmother's driver was taking him to the airstrip to board her private jet. On the drive, Quentin mentally replayed the conversation between him and his grandmother. She was a wise woman and he valued her opinions and advice. He had no doubt she was right in everything she shared with him. Maybe he needed to step all the way back and just leave Eva alone. He had no idea it was that obvious, his internal feelings for her. Like his grandmother said, Eva was a married woman and he didn't need to do anything to jeopardize her marriage. And if Harper Stenberg was as controlling as his grandmother said he was, that was something that could prove detrimental for Eva. He didn't want that.

Once they arrived at the airstrip and he boarded the luxurious Dassault Falcon 900 jet, he laid his head back against the posh leather seat inside and within a short while, drifted off into a light sleep.

6

"Inside everybody's hiding something."
Dido Armstrong

Eva finished dressing, grabbed her handbag, and then put on her Cartier Paris signature sunglasses, one of Harper's *I'm sorry for beating the crap out of you* gifts. They fully covered the deep purple bruise encircling one of her eyes. Her body still had hidden bruises from Harper's brutal beating. Thank God her clothing covered them. She thought he was going to kill her this time—he came close.

With lightning speed, she dashed past the kitchen hoping if Marissa was in there, she wouldn't see her. She paused at the door leading to the three car garage, scanning the perimeter of where she stood, waiting on her fur babies to come barking, something they always did whenever she was about to leave the colossal house.

Not seeing Marissa or her dogs, she shrugged. *Guess they're on Marissa's side of the house.* Sometimes they would hang out with Marissa who had her own area on the east wing of the house. It was what some might call a mother-in-law suite, only on a much grander scale. It was complete with two bedrooms, a large master bath, full kitchen, and living room area.

Inside her car, she touched the screen to pull up her menu options so she could pull up the business she was headed to in Miami.

Eva turned off her street heading toward Adverse City Boulevard, the main thoroughfare. She hadn't spoken to any of the ladies in at least two weeks, and for good reason—Harper. All of their calls and texts went unanswered by her. What would she say to them? She was tired of hiding and lying, but if she answered any of their calls or texts she would have broken down. She didn't want to do that. Every day she tried her best to move past the horror she lived whenever Harper was around. There were moments and times when he treated her like a queen only to turn into a stark raving mad, almost inhuman, person.

Avery was the only housewife she had confided in but even Avery didn't know Harper was still beating up on her. When she first told Avery about it, of course Avery was incensed. She wanted to tell Ryker but Eva insisted that she not do that. It would only set Harper off even more and he would cut off the money he sent to her family. Whenever Avery asked if

Harper had hit her again, Eva did everything she could to convince Avery all was back to normal in the Stenberg household.

As for telling the other housewives, she didn't have the strength or nerve to tell them what she had been going through. She was afraid if she did the word would get out and she would face public humiliation. That was the last thing she wanted or needed, especially if it got back to Quentin. She would be so embarrassed. It was bad enough that she had to stop working for him and that Harper accused her of sleeping with him. How could she have been so naïve as to think Harper wouldn't find out she was working with Quentin? The man had eyes and ears in every place it seemed. As Eva thought about it, she began to have doubts about Quentin. Could he be part of Harper's team? Was his kindness and his offer for her to work with him so she could start making and saving money of her own a farce or some kind of smoke screen? She didn't know who to trust.

"Siri. Call—"

Before she could finish instructing Siri to call Avery, Meesha's name appeared on the vehicle's dash screen. Eva made the quick decision to answer.

"Hi, Meesha."

"Ohmygosh. I can't believe you finally decided to answer. What's going on with you? I've missed you. You haven't returned any of my calls or texts. You okay?"

"Yes, I'm...I'm fine. I've just been busy."

"I've been worried about you. It's good to hear your voice."

"I'm sorry I've been missing in action lately. I haven't talked to any of the housewives. I'm, well Harper wants me to become more involved with his show."

"Oh, that sounds super. Does he want you to showcase more of your heart healthy meals like you did the last time?"

"Pretty much."

"Uhh, you don't sound too excited about it."

"I am, it's just that I'm headed to the studio now and this traffic is crazy."

"Oh, I didn't know you were driving. I'm sorry. I was calling to let you know we're having ladies day out Friday. You in? We're meeting at this new Latin café, Las Olas. "

"I...I don't know. I'll have to get back to you on that."

"Eva, are you sure you're okay? You sound; you sound preoccupied." Meesha was growing concerned. Eva didn't sound at all like herself. She prayed her and Harper weren't having more marital problems. The last time the ladies got together, Eva said things had been pretty good between them. Had things changed?

"I'm okay. I'll call you later, Meesha."

"Okay. I'll talk to you later."

Eva didn't know if she would meet the ladies or not. If her bruises were still visible there was no way she would. She couldn't keep hiding behind her sunglasses.

Ω

Eva arrived at the NW Second Avenue Shop. Before exiting her vehicle, she looked in her rear view mirror and side mirrors as if she was expecting someone to suddenly pull up on her.

Nervous, she sucked in her breath then exhaled it slowly before opening the door and getting out of the car.

Slowly, she walked up to the door, opened it, and walked inside. She gasped when she saw hundreds of firearms all over the small store—some mounted on the walls and others enclosed behind glass cases.

"May I help you," an older black gray-haired man asked.

"Yes, I...I'd like to get a gun."

7

"A house divided cannot stand."
Matthew 12:25, Bible

Meesha left Perfecting Your Faith Academy a few hours earlier than usual. The day had been slow and uneventful so after finishing several of the projects she and her staff had been working on all week, she gathered her things and left for home. She talked to Avery who told her she would bring the boys home for her when she picked up Lexie and Heather from school.

Meesha missed her baby girl. Makena Grace brightened Meesha's life in such a special way. There was no mistaking her sons brought her joy too but they didn't like being kissed and slobbered on like Makena.

She was glad her tortuous nightmares had slowed down tremendously. The last one she had of Terrell and that awful night had been months ago. Thank God they never really woke up Carlton. The last thing she needed was for him to start in on her about being stressed, depressed and overwhelmed and asking a million and one questions about what she had been dreaming about. If he only knew; but she was glad he didn't know what she'd done that fateful night. It was something she would live with and be tormented by the rest of her natural life. She couldn't thank God enough for blessing her with the family she had—her four sons, her little girl, and her husband in spite of the horrible crime she'd committed. That was why she was committed to Perfecting Your Faith and to being the best woman of God she could be. Though the memories of what she'd done often made her feel unworthy of her title and position, First Lady, she struggled to keep them at bay and live her best life—a life God had seen fit to give her. She thanked Him for giving her the chance to start over in her life with renewed opportunities.

When the garage door opened, Meesha saw Carlton's car and a smile immediately rushed to her face. Since Makena Grace's birth, Carlton seemed to take advantage of any excuse to come home to spoil his little princess too. Yes, Makena was definitely the light of all of their lives. Even the boys loved to spoil her, and they never wanted to see her cry.

Entering the house, she laid her keys and purse on the table inside the foyer where she'd entered.

Walking through the kitchen, down the long winding hallway leading toward the stairs, she gave pause when she heard voices emanating from Carlton's office. It was a female's voice. At first she thought it was Yulisa but as she drew closer she realized the voice didn't belong to their nanny.

"So everything is still on?" the woman asked.

Meesha approached the partially opened door.

"Yes, unless something comes up with Meesha and the kids. I don't think anything will. What about—"

Carlton paused when he saw the door opening and there stood Meesha.

"Evelyn? Heyyy. What are you doing here?" Meesha asked, pleasantly surprised.

Carlton, holding Makena in his arms, walked up to his wife and kissed her on the cheek. "Hi, sweetheart. You're home early."

"So are you," Meesha countered and returned his kiss with one on his lips before she started talking to Makena Grace. "But I know why." She smiled again.

"How's mommy's little dumpling?" She kissed her little girl and Makena reached for her. "Evelyn, what's going on with you? I didn't see your car when I drove up." Meesha took her little girl and began talking love talk to her and kissing her. Makena soaked it up and a cute, tiny giggle escaped from their baby girl.

Evelyn walked up to Meesha and embraced her with a side hug. "I'm with your husband. Martin is out of town for the week attending that seminar in Houston. I was bored out of my mind. When Carlton called to check on me and I told him I was about to pull out my weave, he told me he was coming home early to see his little girl, and asked if I wanted him to come by and pick me up. I couldn't pass up the chance to see this sweet little thing. Plus, I told him I was hungry but I didn't want to eat alone. Most of my girlfriends work nine to five so you know how that goes. It's hard to hook up with them."

"Yea, I do. But I told you, we can always use extra hands at the academy, Evelyn. You don't have to be a bored housewife. And you're free to join me and my girlfriends on our ladies day out luncheons."

"I know, and I think I'm going to take you up on that offer to work at the academy sooner than you think. It's just that since I've only stopped working less than a year ago, I was trying to take advantage of being a lady of leisure and a stay at home mom. You know one of those blessed ladies who while the kids are at school can chill, shop, chill, shop, repeat." Evelyn laughed. "But I am definitely not going to hang with you and your lady friends. Their blood is too rich for my veins. I can't keep up with you ladies." Evelyn and Meesha both laughed.

"Okay, ladies. I know where this is leading. You two talk as long as you'd like. I'm going over here and check my emails."

"I'll be ready in a sec, Carlton," Evelyn told him.

Evelyn and Martin had two kids of their own. Martin adored children which was why he had started working with the youth at church. He spent a lot of time with them, arranging field trips, youth conferences, seminars, anything to keep them on the straight and narrow. He always included his sons although they weren't teens yet.

"I miss Martin so much when he's away. I was about to go stir crazy up in that house all by my lonesome. The boys won't be home until much later, which is why I gladly accepted Carlton's offer to get out of that big empty house. I hope you don't mind me latching on to your man."

"And don't forget you wanted to discuss the Pastoral Care Ministry," Carlton reiterated.

"Right."

"Girl, please We're family. I told you, my *casa es su casa*. You're welcome here any time."

Meesha turned toward Carlton. "Honey, I forgot all about the Christian Education Conference just that quick. You *are* still planning to attend the last two days aren't you?"

"Yes, I guess so. That's what Evelyn and I were talking about. She's thinking about going with me to surprise Martin. Hey, why don't you come along too?"

"I would love to but I'm going to pass on this one. It's such short notice for me and I wouldn't put Yulisa on the spot like that. Anyway, I told the boys we would do something fun while you were gone this weekend."

"Okay, maybe next time. I like it when we go together."

"Me too," Meesha replied.

Carlton sighed inwardly, glad his reverse psychology worked. Knowing his wife the way he did, he knew she would renege on accompanying him on the trip. Meaning, he and Evelyn's plans were still in play and the two of them could get in a make out session or two on the trip to Houston."

"Evelyn, I bet Martin is going to get a kick out of seeing you show up at the conference.

That man travels so much for Perfecting Your Faith. I'm sure it will do him good to see his wife."

"Yes, that's what I was telling Carlton. I go with him as often as I can, but you and I know, as does Martin, those conferences and seminars are not my cup of tea. They are so boring and there's only so much shopping a girl can do before I'm back in a hotel room going out of my mind. And when I do sit in on an actual conference, it only takes a minute and I'm ready to go out like a light. Sleep overtakes me. I can't do it. That's why I know I am not meant to be a first lady like you." Evelyn laughed and gave a side eye to Carlton who remained seated at his computer.

"You want to join us for lunch then?" Carlton asked his wife, hoping she would say no to that as well.

"You two go ahead. Enjoy yourselves. I came home early for a reason—to love on this bundle of joy," she kissed Makena again, "and then I'm going to get out of these clothes, shower, and wait on the boys. Avery said she would drop them off."

"Okay, cool, but if she can't you know I have no problem picking them up," Carlton offered.

"It's up to you. Where are you two going for lunch? You know yet?"

Yea, right back to my brother's house and in my brother's bed, he thought. Carlton looked at Evelyn for the answer.

Evelyn shrugged slightly. "Ummm, I hadn't given it much thought. All I know is I'm hungry. I can eat just about anything."

"Okay, on that note, let's go. I don't want you running to my brother complaining about me not looking out for you." Carlton pushed back from his desk, stood up, and walked toward his wife and Evelyn.

"I know that's right," Meesha added and laughed.

"Bye-bye, sweet baby girl." Evelyn lightly kissed Makena on the side of her face while the little girl rested her head against her mother's shoulder.

"So do you want me to get the boys?"

"No, don't worry about it. You two go and have a good time," Meesha said. "I want to see Avery anyway."

"Okay, I'll see you a little later. I love you."

"I love you, too. Bye, Evelyn. Make sure my husband feeds you good."

"You heard that didn't you, brother-in-law?"

Oh, I'm going to feeda all right. "Yea, I heard her. And don't you worry, sweetheart, I plan to give her whatever she wants."

8

*"Some of us think holding on makes us strong;
but sometimes it is letting go." Herman Hess*

"Does anyone know what's up with Eva?"
Peyton asked as they sat at Las Olas.

"I don't know. I told her about today. She
said she would let me know if she was coming,
but I haven't heard from her. And that was
Tuesday when we talked. I don't know what's
going on. When we *did* talk, she sounded a
little weird, like something was on her mind.
Avery, she usually talks to you more than we
do," Meesha said between bites of grilled
vegetables.

"I know, and I've called and texted her but
she hasn't answered me either." Avery was
getting increasingly worried about her friend.

"She mentioned something about Harper
wanting her to spend more time with him
working on his TV show," Meesha said.

"Girl, please, what is she going to do to
help, Harper? That's a bunch of bull," Peyton
said, taking a bite of her Cubana sandwich.
"Harper must be going upside that head."
Peyton covered her mouth as she leaned back

in her chair and started laughing. She didn't mean to laugh because if it really was Harper and Eva she saw fighting in the car not too long ago, then this would be far from a laughing matter. But over time she convinced herself the couple she saw that day hadn't been them.

Avery didn't find it funny because Peyton had no idea about Harper's abusive side. If she *did* no way would she have made such a snide comment. What Peyton said gave her pause to think about it though. Had Harper hit Eva again? Surely he hadn't because Eva would have told her or would she? She had to find out if that was the case whether Eva wanted her to know or not. It was time she came to her best friend's rescue.

"Peyton, you need to stop," cautioned Avery. "You're always talking too dang much. Put a filter on it."

"What did I say? You can't take a joke? Or is Ryker going up side your noggin?" Peyton burst out laughing again and this time she picked up her glass of iced coffee and took a swallow.

Meesha rolled her eyes and shook her head. "Stop it, you two. Seriously, something is going on with Eva. This isn't like her at all. And isn't her graduation from culinary school coming up?"

"Yes." Avery pulled out her phone and looked at her calendar. "It's next Thursday evening."

"If all else fails and we don't hear from her before then, we'll see her then because we're going to be front and center at that graduation. She's going to give us some answers one way or the other. Agreed?" Meesha looked at Avery and Peyton for their approval.

"Agreed," they both said almost in unison.

Ω

Eva left her last culinary class and hurried to her car. It was an exhilarating feeling to know that some good had come out of Harper's insistence that she find a hobby or something to past the time. It led her to fulfill a dream she didn't know she had buried inside. In a week she would walk down the aisle to receive her associates in Culinary Arts. Next step, to secure a job at a restaurant as a pastry chef or maybe even a personal chef. Realistically, however she knew that was nothing more than a pipe dream because as long as she was with Harper, Eva knew there was no way he would allow her to work for anyone. He'd made that perfectly clear.

Walking toward her car, and taking a quick look across the street at the rescue shelter, she hoped she'd missed Quentin the same as the previous three days. The last thing she wanted was for him to walk up on her, but there would be nothing she could do if he did. Luckily, the past few days, she seemed to have dodged him or missed him because he hadn't shown up at her car or at school.

Quentin was a persistent man. He and Harper had that trait in common. The thing about Quentin was he hadn't shown himself to be controlling. He was a kind soul, evident by his gentle nature and love for animals. Yet, he had no problem appearing at the culinary school at the end of her class to check on her and see how she was progressing with her courses. The instructors knew him and admired him for being the master chef he was.

Opening the door and getting inside her car, she took another glance across the street at *Scooby Doo's Rescue Shelter* before pulling out of her parking space and driving into the street. Passing the shelter, she quickly looked to see if she could possibly spot Quentin through the huge picture window. She couldn't. That was a good thing; she didn't need to see him and he didn't need to see her. If he was one of Harper's undercover cronies, it was best that things remain like they were, meaning she needed to stay as far away from him and the shelter as possible.

She looked at the dash when the phone started ringing. "Hi."

"Meet me at the studio," Harper ordered rather than asked.

"I can't. I have things to do. You know my graduation is next week, and I'm just leaving class. I need to—"

"Does it sound like I'm asking? Be here in thirty minutes—at the studio." The dash went clear as he abruptly ended the call.

Eva sighed and continued driving, changing her destination to the direction of the TV studio.

Reluctantly driving to the studio, she thought about her recent trip. What had she been thinking when she walked into that gun store last week? She could never hurt Harper or anyone for that matter. Yes, he beat her up. Yes, he could be mean and cruel, but to think that she had gone so far as to think about purchasing a gun? What was wrong with her? Maybe she needed to talk to someone. She needed counseling. One thing she did know—it couldn't be Carlton Porter. No way. And it couldn't be Quentin either. Although she wondered if he was on Harper's side, something told her Quentin was not that kind of man. He would never betray his friends in that manner. She hoped she was right about him.

Without admitting, not even to herself, her feelings were strong for him, but she had never acted on them. No way could she ever betray Harper again by sleeping with another man. Look where it had gotten her? Their marriage had been basically torn apart. On the outside it may have appeared to be intact, but if only people knew what she suffered at home.

She'd paid the price for her one time indiscretion. The night she let her physical needs overcome her sense of reasoning was the biggest mistake of her life. She hadn't laid eyes on Seth since and she prayed she wouldn't have to ever see him again.

9

"It isn't always a change of scenery needed to make life better. Sometimes it simply requires opening your eyes." R. E. Goodrich

Peyton invited Derek to join her for a romantic stroll along Pointe Beach, and afterward have dinner at Yardbird. He loved the place. She believed it would set the stage for what she wanted to talk to him about. She wasn't getting any younger and if she planned on giving her husband a child, a biological child, she didn't want to waste another minute.

Liam was sixteen years old. It wouldn't be long before he left the house for college. He had been such a blessing in her life, in both of their lives, but deep down inside she was no fool. She knew how much Derek desired to have a biological child of his own. He was the perfect father to Liam. He treated him no different than if Liam *was* his biological son. He was the best father and she had no doubts he would be the perfect father to their child together. The key was getting him on board with her having artificial insemination or in vitro. Would he go for it or would he tell her they should just let sleeping dogs lie? She prayed he would be in agreement with her. This would only strengthen their marriage.

She had stopped drinking, healed from her physical injuries from that horrid accident, and she was moving forward with her life. To seal their union with a child would be the ultimate blessing. She wanted to prove to Derek that he was the man, the only man, for her. They had money, money, and more money. Why not use some of it, which would be like pocket change to them, to help bring a child of their own into the world.

"Derek, will you be home soon?"

Derek sat behind his desk in his office at Adverse City Bank going through some files his administrative assistant left on his computer.

"I don't know. I'm trying to get out of here but I still have some things I need to finish up. It may be a couple more hours. Why? What's going on?"

"I thought we could go for a walk on Pointe Beach and afterwards I'd like to take you to dinner. You work so hard. You need a break, don't you think?"

Derek was somewhat flattered. Peyton could be a sweetheart when she wanted to. Sure, they'd had their share, more than their share, of ups and downs in their marriage but he had listened to God and remained in it. Plus, he would never want to leave his son without a father in the home. He couldn't do that to Liam. Yes, Liam was a young adult, but that only meant he needed a father even more. He sometimes, well, he often thought about him and Peyton having a child. But he told himself to get that out of his mind. Obviously, it hadn't been God's will so he had basically come to terms with it years ago. However, it didn't stop him from thinking about *what if*. Maybe their lives would have been totally different had she been able to give him a kid. But it wasn't to be and he had learned to live with it. Or had he?

Now that his wife had stopped drinking, things were so much better on the home front. But that's how it always was when she stopped drinking. The thing is, it never lasted more than a year, and then Peyton would go back to her drinking ways. He prayed this time would be different.

"I don't know how much longer I'll be here."

"Derek, come on. Whatever it is you're doing, you can do it from your home office. Better still, it can wait until tomorrow. Well, tomorrow is Saturday. But that doesn't matter; you still can work on it tomorrow. Can't you?"

Pause. Silence.

"I want to spend time with you. Liam is at church at the youth lock-in. We have the whole

63

night to ourselves," she semi-pleaded. "and there's something important I need to talk to you about."

Derek shifted in his chair as he listened to his wife's request. He had told himself he should make a conscientious effort to be more present in the marriage. What he was doing at work *could* wait, just as Peyton said.

"What is it you want to talk about?" he asked, without committing to leaving the bank and going home.

"Don't make me beg, Derek."

Derek began to detect the frustration in her voice and he relented. "You know what? You're right. What I'm doing can wait. I'll work on it from home or come back to the bank tomorrow and finish up."

A smile formed on Peyton's lips. *Yes! He's coming.* "Okay, I'll see you soon."

"Yeah, just let me clear up some things on my desk and I'll be on my way. And you know what?"

"What?"

"I *am* hungry. I barely took time to eat lunch. It's been wild today. Meeting after meeting. One situation after another."

"Well, just come home. I'll be waiting."

Ω

The walk along Pointe Beach was magical and romantic. They walked along the white sandy beach barefoot, stopping only briefly to watch the beautiful waves. There were several surfers on the water.

"Wish you were out there, don't you?"

"Yeah, I do."

"Derek, you should take more time out to do the things you love to do. You rarely go surfing anymore, and Liam loves it too. I'm so glad you taught him.

"I am too. He goes surfing more than I do with his friends." Derek stopped and watched the surfers and smiled.

Peyton clung to his hand and watched along with him. The sun began to set. It was gorgeous and they sat on the beach in the sand enjoying the beauty of God's majestic creation.

"This is like heaven," Derek said. "I feel so at peace. I'm glad you thought of this, sweetheart." He kissed Peyton on her cheek and she turned toward him. Their lips united in a deep passionate kiss.

Ω

On the drive to the restaurant, Derek tried to get Peyton to tell him what she wanted to talk to him about but she refused.

"I don't want to talk about it in the car. Let's wait until we get to the restaurant, order our food, and then we can talk. Let's not rush anything tonight."

"Ohhh...kay." Derek smiled. "Umm, you're killing me woman. I want to know what's happening."

"All I'm tellin' you is it's nothing bad. I hope you'll just hear me out and then be on board with me. Now, enough talk about what it is I have to tell you. Let's talk about your son."

"What about him?"

"You know he has a new girlfriend, don't you?" Peyton said, changing the subject entirely.

"Yeah, I know. And I think he really likes this one, which is why I stay on him about carrying an umbrella with him at all times."

"Derek! Please, I can't imagine Liam having sex with some little fass tail girl. Not my baby."

"He's not a baby anymore, Peyton. And unless you want to become a grandmother at an early age, I suggest you start talking to him too about the same girls you call *fass*. I want him to know what's up out there. He's sixteen years old. He's smart, handsome, popular, and he comes from a wealthy, very wealthy family. The girls are after him. I don't want him slipping."

Peyton nodded. "You're right. You're such an amazing father." She leaned over and kissed him on the cheek.

"Thanks, babe." Derek blushed and reached over and squeezed Peyton's upper thigh, quickly looking over and giving her a sexy smile.

Derek and Peyton went to Yardbird Southern Table and Bar in Miami. They'd only been there twice since the night of the accident. Things were different, far different for her since that troubled time in her life. Staying away from alcohol had changed her entire perspective on life, motherhood, and her marriage. She continued to attend AA meetings once a month and she remained in contact with her counselor. All was going right, which is why she prayed tonight would replace old memories with fresh, new and good memories for her and Derek.

Derek loved Yardbird. The place was always packed but he didn't mind the wait because the food was always on point. Tonight, Peyton had made reservations for the two of them so they didn't have to wait.

The hostess led them to their table. While they waited on their server they perused the menu.

A young man appeared shortly after they were seated. "Hi, my name is Horace. I'll be your server. What can I get you to drink?"

"I'd like a virgin southern peach," Peyton answered.

Out of respect for his wife and because he understood her struggle, Derek ordered a virgin drink for himself. "I'll have the virgin banana walnut."

"I'll be back with your drinks and then I'll take your orders."

"Thank you," Derek said."

"Oh, excuse me, may we have two waters with lemon too?" asked Peyton.

"Sure, the server stated before turning and walking away.

The couple laughed, talked about church, things going on at the bank, and discussed their son some more while they waited on their food to arrive.

The server returned with their appetizers. They shared whole roasted cauliflower with pickled mustard seed chimichurri.

While they enjoyed the delicious cuisine and waited on their entrees, Peyton carefully approached the subject of her desire to have a child.

At first mention, Derek picked up his glass of water and took a big gulp before releasing a light cough.

"A baby? You want to have a baby? My God, Liam is sixteen years old, Peyton."

"Yes, he is, but I'm still a young woman. Not quite forty. And I know you want a child. I mean, yes you're the best father a kid could have. Liam is blessed to have you, but I know you've always wanted a child of your own. And there's no reason you shouldn't have one."

"But you haven't gotten pregnant in all these years. What makes you think you can all of a sudden get pregnant now? We've done nothing to avoid it and yet..."

"And yet I've never been pregnant. I get it. But I'm no fool either. I've been an alcoholic for many years of our marriage. I'm not saying that it's kept me from getting pregnant, but I think it's contributed to it. Anyway, our marriage is more solid than it's been in years, Derek. I'm no longer drinking and I promise you I will never take another drink for as long as I live. So I want to give you a baby and I want a baby, too. You said it yourself; our son is almost grown. He'll be leaving home for college soon. We're still young and this would be such a blessing, having a little one around. Every time I see Avery and Meesha's little ones,

69

I realize how much I'd like us to experience having a child together."

"But, I've been in Liam's life since he was a toddler."

"I know, but you're not going to sit here and tell me that you wouldn't want to hold a child that you made in your arms."

Derek took a forkful of the cauliflower. As much as he wished he could deny it, he couldn't. Peyton was right; it would be amazing to have a child who had his DNA, his features, his looks. But he believed that was impossible.

Peyton took a final bite of the cauliflower just as the server returned with their entrees.

"Ummm, this looks delicious," she told Derek as the server placed her cornmeal-dusted catfish and sides on the table.

"It sure does," Derek agreed as the server set his St. Louis style pork ribs and sides in front of him.

"Can I get you anything else?"

"No, thank you," Derek replied.

The server walked away and after taking several bites of their food, oohing and aahing in between bites, they resumed their conversation.

"So, tell me, what makes you think if you haven't gotten pregnant in all of these years, things will be different now? Do you think because you've stopped drinking you'll magically get pregnant? I mean, think about it, sweetheart. I don't mean to burst your bubble, but you haven't gotten pregnant and look how long it's been since you've stopped drinking. I'm just saying."

"I know, but I didn't want to tell you anything until I had more information." Peyton took a bite of her side order of farro and roasted root vegetables. "This is the first time I've ordered the farro and roasted vegetables. This is divine."

Derek reached over with his fork and took a forkful of the veggies and placed it inside his mouth.

"Umm, that *is* good. Not once have we come here and the service and food wasn't good. Here, taste these brussels."

Peyton did as Derek had done and took her fork to get a forkful of his brussels.

"Yum," she said.

While she chewed her food, he took a bite of his cheesy skillet cornbread before he returned to the subject at hand.

"So what is this information you have?" he asked, curiously, while eating and then picking up his glass of water.

"Well, I went to see a fertility specialist."

Derek stopped chewing his food. "You what?"

"Yes, I didn't want to tell you because if I didn't hear what I hoped and prayed I would hear, I didn't want you to be disappointed. But, it wasn't like that at all."

"When did you do this?"

"A couple of weeks ago."

"And you're just telling me now?"

"Yes. I had a follow-up appointment and I wanted to study up on what the doctor told me before I came to you. Are you upset?"

"No, I just wish you had told me. I would have gone with you."

Peyton smiled, reached over the table, and grabbed Derek's hand that rested next to his plate of food. "I'm glad to hear that."

"So what did this specialist have to say?"

"Well," Peyton became almost giddy, "he said...." and Peyton told Ryker everything the specialist told her about first trying artificial insemination. "And if that doesn't work then we can do in vitro."

Derek listened fully. He watched Peyton, saw the glow appear on her face while she explained to him in detail the procedures for her getting pregnant. The more he listened and the more he saw her excitement, the more excited he became. Maybe this *could* work.

Maybe God was going to extend even more favor on their lives and in their marriage.

"So what do you think? You're awfully quiet." She slowly put a forkful of catfish into her mouth.

"I've been listening. I...I have to say, everything you've told me sounds...well, it sounds exciting."

Peyton almost squealed but covered her mouth to stifle it. It sounded as if Derek was on board and she couldn't be happier. God was actually going to give her another chance to make her marriage even stronger. He was definitely a God of second chances and third ones too. She could barely contain herself. This was more than she could ever have expected.

"Before I agree to try this, I'd like to talk to this fertility specialist. I want to know what risks, if any, you might face."

"She did say women like me in their late thirties are at a higher risk of infertility. This risk increases as women reach age forty. She's done tests and thinks I'll make a good candidate. But we can go together and you can ask her whatever you want to ask. Oh, Derek, I'm so happy. I'll make the appointment. I can't believe it. We might be having our own baby! Wait until I tell Liam."

"I wouldn't tell Liam just yet. Let's wait to see how this is going to pan out."

"Honey, you've said it yourself; Liam is not a baby anymore. I think he deserves to know what our plans are. We're a family."

"Yes, and you're right, but I'd like to wait to talk to him until after you and I see the specialist together. Okay?"

"Okay." Placing her hand over her chest, she exhaled and smiled again. "I think this calls for dessert. What do you say? Do you have enough room?"

"I couldn't agree with you more. But before we order dessert, what do you say we have a toast."

Derek raised his glass of banana walnut and it met Peyton's southern peach drink. "To our future. To all God has in store for the Hudson family."

"Yes," Peyton agreed, "to the Hudsons."

10

"From the deepest desires often comes the deadliest hate." Socrates

"Okay, enough is a enough. I want to know the reason you refuse to go to church with me and the kids? And don't give me that lame excuse again about you're taking a break. It's been months since you've been to Perfecting Your Faith. So tell me, what's the real reason, Avery? And don't shuck and jive me. I want to know the truth."

"I don't know what you want me to say other than I'm just not feeling it anymore. I mean, I listen to Carlton preach the same old messages. It's like all he's doing is a remix, the same way some singers do with their songs. Plus, I know God for myself. There's nothing else he can tell me that I don't already know."

Ryker wasn't buying it. There was something else going on with his wife. He didn't know if she and Meesha had exchanged words or if she was into it with one of her other housewife friends or somebody at church. As a lawyer, he was rigged to see behind a person's words and determine whether they were telling the truth, hiding something, or just holding back. Avery was holding back and hiding something. What it was, he needed to find out.

"Forget about being tired of hearing what Pastor Porter has to say. I want you to go with me and the girls. I don't see how two hours of your time on a Sunday morning can hurt you. Especially when it means fellowshipping with your family. The girls, and RJ too, need to see us united as one when it comes to our spiritual beliefs. You staying at home Sunday after Sunday does not set a good example."

Avery raised both hands in the air as a sign of surrender. "Okay, okay. I'll go to church tomorrow. But I'm telling you, don't expect me to start back going with you every Sunday."

"And I'm saying, I do *want* and hope you would come with us every Sunday. That is, unless you or one of the kids are sick or something. Or maybe if we've agreed as husband and wife not to go on a particular Sunday. I don't pressure you about attending mid-week service because often I'm unable to make it myself because of my schedule, but Sunday....no excuse. Okay?"

Avery scooped up her legs on the sofa, slightly rolled her eyes, and tilted her head. "Okay, Ryker. If it'll keep peace around here, I guess I'll go."

Ryker got up from his chair and walked over and sat down next to his wife. He wrapped an arm around her, turned her head toward him, and kissed her.

"Whaddaya say we turn in early?"

Avery pulled back slightly and looked curiously at her husband. "Ryker, it's only seven o'clock."

"So? That gives us the whole night to—"

"To what?"

"To do this." He pulled Avery into his arms. He started out with a tender slow kiss then forced her lips open with his thrusting tongue. The kiss sent the pit of her stomach into a wild swirl.

Momentarily, he pulled back, stood up, and took her hand. She didn't put up a protest as she allowed him to lead her toward the stairs. At the foot of the stairs he surprised her with another kiss. This one a slow, drugging kiss that sent shivers of delight that roused her passion.

Ryker further surprised her when he swept her, weightless, into his arms and carried her up the winding staircase to their bedroom.

At that moment, Avery threw caution to the wind. She didn't think about the girls, about RJ or anything else. Having a nanny around twenty four/seven was a good thing. Thank God for lots of money and blessings.

Ryker gently placed her on the bed and began removing her clothing. When Avery tried to speak, he placed a finger over her lips.

"I've got this," he said softly but hungrily. He continued removing her clothes until she was as naked as the day she came into the world. He looked at her with so much desire it almost made Avery a little self-conscious. Was he staring at her imperfect body? She'd bore three children. Her body was far less than perfect like it used to be in her call girl days.

He must have read her thoughts because he said before he leaned in and kissed her. "You're beautiful."

Ryker quickly undressed, throwing his clothes across the bed, the same as he did with hers. His tongue caressed her sensitive swollen mounds as his hands slid across her belly. Instinctively, her body arched to meet his as she implored him with her eyes. He kissed her again and again between his whispers of love for each part of her body.

Avery clung to her husband like he was a life preserver on a stormy sea. This was what she craved, love and affection unconditionally. How could she have ever thought Carlton Porter would have been that man? She almost ruined her marriage and her family with her insecurities and own driving needs.

Her heart swelled with feelings for Ryker she thought were dead. Thank God for miracles. Thank God for saving her from herself and giving her another chance to commit herself to her husband and children.

"I love you, Avery. I really do love you," Ryker whispered hoarsely.

She couldn't deny it any longer. She pulled her drifting thoughts together and allowed herself to be drawn to a height of passion she had not experienced in a long time.

11

"We fear our enemy but the bigger and real fear is that of someone who is sweetest to your face and most vile behind your back." Mufti Menk

Meesha praised God and stood to her feet. The choir was on fire this morning. Hands in the air and jumping up and down, Meesha screamed, "Hallelujah. Praise you God. You are worthy." On and on she went as she was consumed by a spiritual high.

The other housewives sat two or three pews behind Meesha who was seated on the reserved second row of the purple pews.

Peyton looked extremely happy, grateful Derek wanted to give artificial insemination a try. Her life was changing for the better and she couldn't be happier than she was right now.

Eva—quite the opposite. She sat next to Harper who had a tight grip of her hand like she was a child trying to escape from their parent. The TV taping had gone well. Whenever she was able to prepare food it gave her an odd sense of peace. If Harper was the Harper she first met then things would be perfect, but he wasn't and now she had changed too. She couldn't wait until her graduation. Somehow, someway she would have to find a way to move forward and to get away from Harper, even if that meant she might have to leave Adverse City.

Avery sat next to Ryker, him holding her hand and kneading it. If joining her husband in church was what he desired of her, she told herself she had to swallow her fears and her contempt for Carlton, and put on a happy face for her husband. She didn't want to lose this feeling, this growing closeness in their marriage—and definitely not because of the likes of a vile person like the man approaching the pulpit.

Carlton walked up to the podium in the pulpit after the last song by the choir. "Praise the Lord," he exclaimed. "Let's praise him!"

The people in the congregation clapped, praised God, and many stood to their feet. The organist began playing a chord that caused many of them to start doing their own 'holy dances'. Some looked like the dances they did in the nightclub, but nevertheless, they danced and Carlton took it all in.

He was on a spiritual high himself thinking about the manifold blessings in his life. He looked out over the sanctuary, in awe of the overflow of people in front of him, in the balconies, and on the screen showing those in the overflow room.

Continuing to scan the sanctuary, he saw his wife, his brother Kingston and his new bride, and then his eyes locked in on Evelyn and his brother, Martin. He tried to dispel the thoughts of their recent trip to Houston and even more recent this past Friday night, but found it almost impossible. He and Evelyn had enjoyed their time together while his brother was participating in the youth lock-in at church, and Meesha was at home being the wonderful mom she was. Did he feel any amount of guilt? He couldn't say he did. He was a man with sexual needs that couldn't be tamed or brought into subjection by one woman. And Meesha, let's just say she was willing to experiment in the privacy of their bedroom so he couldn't be more pleased with their lovemaking. Yet, he always yearned for more.

He almost destroyed his marriage when he fell for Avery but thank God, God still showed him some mercy by revealing to him the broad was looney tunes. Then she had the audacity to try to pin Ryker's kid on him. He'd already had to have a DNA test for Liam, but that was different. He was ready to accept the kid if he had been his, but he wasn't the boy's father and that in and of itself was another show of favor from God. He had to start exercising more caution like he did with Evelyn—most of the time, that is. They practiced safe sex seventy five percent of the time but it just wasn't the same as when they went au naturele. But it was different with Evelyn. Carlton fully trusted Evelyn. She had just as much to lose as he did if Martin found out about her indiscretions. She loved her husband and Carlton loved Meesha. It's just they were two wild ones whose spouses couldn't contain them or fully satisfy them.

Evelyn smiled when she saw Carlton looking at her. Friday night was all that and more. He had made love to her like there was no tomorrow. Talking about whip appeal—the boy laid it on her. Stains of scarlet appeared on her cheeks when she replayed the images of their time together. Among these emotions was a small feeling of shame for cheating on Martin.

She looked up at her husband standing up, arms raised, praising God. Her thoughts were racing dangerously. A hot tear rolled down her cheek and she reverted her stare from her husband back to Carlton who was now looking in another direction. If only she could tell herself she would not see Carlton again, but that would be a lie. She actually began trembling.

Martin looked down at his wife and sat back down beside her, wrapping his arm around her shoulder and pulling her into his bosom to comfort her. The Holy Spirit in Perfecting Your Faith was at an all-time high and Martin assumed his wife had been touched by it too. If only he could read her thoughts he would know different and it would utterly destroy him.

Ω

"Honey, you did that thang today." Meesha praised her man. "The church was on fire. The choir sang their hearts out. I'm telling you the spirit of God filled Perfecting Your Faith today."

Carlton sat at the restaurant table with Meesha, the kids, Martin, Evelyn, and his other brother, Kingston and his new bride, Damica. "Yes, God most definitely showed up and showed out."

"Yes, he did," Martin confirmed.

"You always deliver a powerful message but today, bruh, it was like a match had been lit under you," said Kingston as the ladies nodded in agreement.

Makena Grace shuffled from arm to arm while the Porter boys and their families enjoyed eating the delicious Italian cuisine.

Carlton cut eyes at Evelyn and the two exchanged private thoughts about their sizzling affair.

Carlton reached underneath the table and squeezed his wife's thigh while thinking about Evelyn and the shapely beauty of her naked body beneath him. He remembered how she lay panting, her chest heaving, as they satisfied their desires with each other.

"Thanks. It wasn't me. It was God and the Holy Spirit today," Carlton spoke up, addressing the praise of his brothers and family. "I can't do any of what I do without God."

Meesha kissed her husband's cheek. "You're so modest and humble."

Makena was now back in her mommy's arms, but not for long because she reached for her daddy.

Carlton took hold of her, kissed her on her chubby cheeks, and loved on his little girl. All was right and perfect in his world—for now.

12

"There is nothing on this earth more to be prized than true friendship." Thomas Aquinas

Meesha, Peyton, and Avery occupied front and center seats in the mid-size space. They chatted and people watched like they were on an episode of Fashion Police or TMZ.

The hotel's ballroom had been transformed appropriately for Eva's graduation. The class of graduates was small, with no more than twenty people who had completed the costly, private classes offered by Adverse City's elite culinary school.

"I don't see Harper," Avery said to the other housewives, looking around the space as people filed in and took their seats.

Meesha and Peyton looked around the room too but Avery was right, Harper was nowhere in sight.

"I'm sure he'll be here any minute. You know how busy that man is," Meesha said, "but you know he is not about to miss his wife's graduation. Like us, he knows how important this is to Eva."

Peyton rolled her eyes and shook her head. "Y'all act like you're so blind. That man doesn't give two cents about Eva. I'm telling you, things haven't been the same since she screw—I mean, since she slept with his son."

"You're wrong, Peyton. Do you think he would have gone to get her after he put her out? He went to that hotel, packed up her things, and brought her back home. He didn't have to do that if he didn't care about her—if he didn't love her."

Peyton threw up a hand and shook her head again. "You're so naïve, Meesha. That was nothing but game. All he wants to do is save face. Did you see how miserable she looked at church Sunday? She looked like she'd lost her only friend."

"Stop it, just leave it alone, won't you!" Avery seethed.

"Girl, what's your problem?" Peyton asked. "I know she's your best buddy and all, but no need to get your panties stuck in a wedge. We're just talking."

"No, you're doing more than just talking," Avery said, "and like you always do, you're talking too much about something you know nothing about."

The music began to play and the three women stopped talking and focused ahead as someone dressed in full chef's attire approached the raised stage.

Cell phones and video cameras filmed and took pictures of the graduates throughout the two-hour graduation.

Peyton continued looking around to see if she saw Harper. The ladies didn't agree with her, but she didn't really care—she knew something was not right in the Stenberg household. But, hey, if Eva was happy to stay and deal with whatever it was who was she to put up a fuss. To each his own. She had her own business to tend to—giving Derek a baby.

She thought about the night's magical events which transpired after they left Yardbird and went home. Derek was on cloud nine and so was she, after he listened attentively to what she had to share about her visit with the fertility specialist. Hearing and seeing how excited he was at the possibility of them getting pregnant was more than Peyton could imagine.

On the way home, they listened to his playlist of sensual, romantic songs which put both of them in a highly romantic mood. When they pulled into the garage at home, before they got out of the car, Derek leaned over, pulled his wife to him, pressed his lips to hers, caressing her mouth more than kissing it.

When they finally broke apart and went inside, he led her to their bedroom and ordered her to undress.

Peyton liked this Derek. She loved it when he showered her with attention. He eyed her like she was a piece of his favorite candy.

They showered together. His touch was light yet intense. The gentle massage he gave her in the shower sent currents of desire through her.

In their bedroom on their king bed, waves of ecstasy throbbed through her as she welcomed him into her body.

The night was magical. If she had to rate it, she would give it a perfect score.

"Eva doesn't look too happy standing up there. What do y'all think?" Avery whispered.

"I'm not saying," Peyton whispered back so people in front and behind them wouldn't overhear their conversation. "I tried to tell y'all something's not right. And I still don't see Harper." Peyton looked over her shoulder again. This time she did see Harper. He was standing at the back of the ballroom in the doorway. "Wait, look, there he is."

Meesha turned around and her and Harper's eyes met. She quickly turned away and looked back toward the front. "Thank God, he's here. Maybe that's why she was looking all weird. She was probably wondering where he was."

"Yeah, right," said Peyton.

When the ceremony was over, the housewives sought Eva to extend their personal congratulations.

"Thank you for coming," Eva said as Harper stood beside her with his hand around her waist.

"Girl, please. You know we wouldn't have missed this for anything in the world," Avery said and embraced her friend.

"Yes, you know we've got your back. Always will. We're so happy for you. Now we can't wait for you to prepare a full course meal." Meesha and the girls laughed.

"I'm so proud of my wife," Harper said to the ladies and kissed Eva on top of her head. "Did she tell you she's going to be a regular on my show?"

Peyton cut her eyes again but Avery and Meesha acted overjoyed.

"Yes, she told us," Meesha replied. "I know God is going to bless her to do great things."

"Thank you, Meesha," Eva said timidly.

Marissa was also there. She had come to care for Eva like a daughter. She stood with the ladies and with Harper. *Feliz tan feliz, Señora Stenberg* (happy, so happy).

"Thank you, Marissa." Eva took a step forward and embraced her.

Ω

Eva and Marissa, who rode to the graduation with Eva, stepped inside the house just ahead of Harper.

"Mommy's home," Eva said as she walked into the kitchen, surprised her dogs weren't at the door barking to greet her. She was used to them greeting her immediately whenever she walked into the house. This evening was different. The house was eerily quiet.

"I wonder where the dogs are?" she turned and asked Marissa as Harper walked in shortly after.

"I do not know."

"Maybe they're asleep," said Eva. "I didn't put them in their kennels before I left. Did you, Marissa?"

"No, Senora."

Eva turned and looked at Harper. "Did you come home before you came to the graduation?"

"Yes, as a matter of fact I did."

"Did you see the dogs?"

Harper nodded. "I have a surprise."

"A surprise? What kind of a surprise?" Suddenly Eva didn't feel right. Something was going on. What had Harper done?

"Yes, now that you've completed culinary school and you'll be working with me, I know the dogs are a lot to deal with. You won't have time to take care of them like you used to, and Marissa," he looked at Marissa with a smile plastered on his face, "already has a full plate."

"Where are my babies, Harper?" Eva asked, growing uneasy.

Marissa looked on in total despair, knowing Dr. Stenberg had done something that was not right. She had heard and practically witnessed his mistreatment of Eva but there was nothing she could do about it. She was an employee, an illegal immigrant at that, who Harper had brought into his home, paid her extremely well, and provided a roof over her head in their huge home. She could never go against him or she might be sent back to Mexico and suffer all kind of ill treatment. She had no family, no one to care for her except for Harper Stenberg. He was always a good man, but something changed in him a year or two into his marriage to the young, beautiful Eva.

"I asked you a question, Harper. Where are my dogs?" Eva fumed as her voice escalated and her brows drew downward in a frown.

He shot her a twisted smile. "I rehomed them. They're with someone who has the time to provide the care they need. Don't worry, the family I gave them to love animals. As a matter of fact, they're animal advocates and vegans so you can be sure they'll take good care of them."

Eva's full hazel eyes darkened as she boldly met his eyes. She walked up on him and began pounding him on his chest as tears poured from her eyes. "How could you? Tell me where they are. Tell me who you gave my babies too! Tell me, Harper. Tell me now," she continued screaming until she went down on her knees.

Harper turned to Marissa. "Marissa, if you don't mind we need to be alone."

"Yes, Senor Harper," and reluctantly Marissa walked away toward her wing of the house, feeling bad for Eva and angry over how cruel Dr. Stenberg was to give Eva's dogs away. He knew how much she loved those pups. How could he be so mean?

Weeping uncontrollably on the floor, Eva's stomach muscles clinched tightly. She gasped, panting in terror.

"For God's sake—enough, Eva. It's not the end of the world. Stop being so darn dramatic." His voice was absolutely emotionless. He reached down and pulled her up with force. "Get up. You're such a diva. If anyone was to see how you're behaving they wouldn't be able to tell you were nothing but poor Bolivian trash when I found you. Come on, settle down, have something to eat, and we can talk about your next move since you've graduated. You're always talking about us not spending much time together. Well, now that you're done with school and you're not wasting your time at that god awful animal place Emma Winters' grandson owns, then we can spend more time together. I can't wait to see what other dishes you're going to conjure up for the show."

What was wrong with this man? He talked and acted like he hadn't just ripped a hole in her heart. He'd taken away the very things she loved. How could he? How could a person be so cruel to another person? Especially toward a person he professed to have undying love for.

Eva pulled herself out of his clutches and took off upstairs. Instead of going to their bedroom, she ran to the room where she kept her dogs, hoping and praying it was a cruel prank Harper was playing and she would find her dogs in the room. Their kennels were gone, their dog beds, doggy toys, everything was gone. He had really given them away.

Surprisingly, Harper didn't follow her. For that, she was glad. She couldn't take another one of his beatings. She spent the night in the room curled on the bed. The whole night she wept on and off as sleep escaped her. Just thinking about what he'd done repeatedly stabbed at her heart. She breathed in shallow, quick gasps as if a hand had closed around her throat. *Why, why, why oh, God didn't I buy that gun?*

Ω

Over the next few days, Marissa tried to do whatever she could to console Eva but there was little she could do to comfort her and make her feel better. One day she even prepared Eva's favorite Bolivian meal, silpancho, a dish made up of rice, golden potatoes, beef, fried eggs and topped with onion and tomato salsa.

"Senora Eva, please eat. I made silpancho, *tu favorito* (your favorite)."

Curled up on the bed, she barely raised her head. "Thanks, Marissa. I'm not hungry. Maybe later."

"What can I do...to help," Marissa asked in broken English, "to make you better?"

Eva lifted her head and with a grim look on her face she said, "*Mátalo.*" (Kill him).

13

"One of the hardest things in life is to be brave enough to be yourself." Bradley Cooper

Two weeks had gone by since Eva's graduation. The ladies had called and texted but just like she did the last time they tried reaching her, she ignored them. Her heart was broken. She barely ate and she spent most of the time in the room where her dogs were usually kept.

Not having the little pooches around was like losing her children. The text notifier pinged and this time she slowly looked at it and a smile flooded her face. It was a text from Quentin.

"hru?"

Eva looked at the text like he had written a short story. She allowed her mind to reflect on the good times she had whenever she was around Quentin. Why couldn't it be that way with Harper? Quentin seemed to be everything Harper was not.

Just as she was about to reply, she stopped as that feeling of mistrust crept up on her instantly. Was he one of Harper's guys? Could this be him trying to bait her in and then run and tell Harper? She didn't know if she should take the chance so she decided to delete his text and not answer. *Better safe than sorry,* something she'd heard Peyton or Meesha say a time or two.

What if Quentin *was* on her side? What if he *did* mean her well? Oh how she wished she could believe that, but memories of Harper's abuse kept her from entertaining good thoughts of Quentin.

The text chimed again. Her heart fluttered as she thought it might have been Quentin again. It was not. It was Meesha.

"Ladies Day Out Thursday. 12:30. Please come. We're going to meet at Full Bloom. I can pick you up if you don't want to drive."

This time Eva decided to respond to the text. Truth be told, she needed to be surrounded by her friends or else she didn't know what she would do. Maybe it was time to tell them the truth about what was going on in her life.

"I'm in," Eva texted and left it at that. She laid her phone to the side and walked out of the bedroom toward her and Harper's bedroom. Shuffling in her closet, she settled on a cute coral colored midi and a pair of platform sandals.

After getting dressed, she chose one of her designer handbags, placed some items from her other bag into the one she was going to carry, and then going back to the dog's room, she got her cell phone.

Downstairs, she ventured into the kitchen. Marissa was not around. Eva opened the door to the garage, walked to her car, got inside, and with a push of the overhead remote, the garage door opened and Eva maneuvered out of the driveway until she was pulling out onto the street.

She drove aimlessly around Adverse City. Without noticing the time and where she was headed, she ended up in the vicinity of her catering school and the rescue shop. As she approached the area, she quickly looked over at the shop. Was Quentin inside? She refused to stop, afraid she might run into him. That was something she did not need to do. Her feelings were all over the place and if she saw him she didn't know how she would respond. Harper had made her so insecure and frankly terrified. The last thing she wanted was him to lay hands on her again.

Driving slowly pass the rescue shop she almost came to a complete stop, crooking her neck and head while trying to get a good look into the shop's large window. She didn't see him, only a few people standing around inside.

No one looked like Quentin. Her phone rang as she drove on by.

Looking at the number on her display screen she frowned when she saw Harper's name appear.

Pushing the button on her steering wheel, she answered the call on speaker.

"Yes," she said nonchalantly, sounding more bothered than anything.

"Where are you?"

"Headed to see Avery," she lied.

"It's about time you got out of the house and stop acting like you lost your best friend. Don't be gone all evening."

"And why not? It's not like I have a reason to come home."

"Why not? Is that what you just asked me? Look, don't try me, Eva. Anyway we're going to meet some important people in the television industry for dinner this evening."

"And what does that have to do with me? That's your thing, not mine."

It was like Harper totally dismissed her feelings and the aggravation in her voice. "My agent called a few days ago while you were holed up in that room sulking over those fur rats. She pitched an idea to some producers. I might get my own reality show." His voice rang with excitement while Eva remained uninterested about what he had going on in his life.

"Isn't that exciting, sweetheart?"

Eva barely replied, "Whatever, Harper."

"So I need you to be on your best behavior. While you're hanging with that delusional friend of yours, why don't you and her go shopping? Buy yourself something real nice to wear. I'll see you in a couple of hours."

Eva watched as the dash screen went blank. Harper had ended the call, leaving her no time to respond.

How much more could she withstand? Now Harper was dictating her every move. Planning her time and beating and threatening her if she refused him. Even their sex life had become emotionless. How could he expect her to desire him and want him to touch her when he did the things he did to her? Yet, in his own warped mind, that's exactly what he expected. If she didn't respond to his touch and lovemaking in the way he thought she should, then he had something to say, which primarily meant he would accuse her of cheating. Eva learned how to make the motions and sounds to keep him satisfied but her mind, body and spirit were not part of it. Lovemaking had become a chore and another way of Harper to exert his power and control.

As she continued driving through the city, she arrived at the Beach Club, Adverse City's exclusive private club where Harper was a member along with the other housewives and their hubbies. She was about to park her vehicle when Avery's number popped up on the dash screen.

"Hey, girl. It's about time you answered your phone."

"Hey, Avery." No matter how she wanted to, Eva couldn't sound as enthusiastic as her best friend. How could she when her life was in shambles? As much as she hated to admit it, she could now fully understand Avery's attempt at taking her own life. Eva felt the same. If it wasn't for her family back in Bolivia, she had no doubt she would have taken herself out. That's just how much she hated her life now. All the money Harper had, the big house, the fancy cars, her high end credit cards, any designer fashion, jewels, and accessories she wanted could not make her happy.

"Why do you sound so down?"

"I'm good."

"Where are you?"

"The Beach Club." Still her voice sounded less than enthusiastic. The day was gorgeous. The weather perfect, the temperatures just right—the perfect time for a stroll.

"Oh, cool. It's been a minute since I've been to the club; I have a free afternoon. I can meet you there if you'd like. We haven't had our own private girl's time in a while."

"I was only going to take a short walk so today is not a good time. It wouldn't make sense for you to come. By the time you got here I would be leaving. Harper and I have a dinner engagement with some high profile television producers. I was just going to take a quick walk and head back to the house."

"Well, can't you at least stop by here for a minute? I miss my best friend."

Eva gave pause and thought about Avery's invitation. She decided to accept it. A visit with Avery might do her some good. Avery was the one person she felt she could truly trust. Of course Meesha and Peyton were trustworthy too but there were some things she withheld from them that she wouldn't keep from Avery.

"Okay. I'll do this another time. I'll be there in about ten minutes or so. Is that okay?"

"Yes. I can't wait to see you."

Ω

"You can't stay in a relationship where a person is abusing you, Eva. And for him to be so cruel as to give your dogs away, knowing how much you loved them? They were like your children. Oh, my God, this is insane. I can't believe you haven't come to me before now."

Eva cried in Avery's arms as Avery tried to console her friend. How could someone, another human being, treat a person the way Harper was treating Eva?

"I don't know what to do," she sobbed.

"You have to get away from him. That's what you have to do. Please let me talk to Ryker, Eva. Please. He can help you. He'll know what to do."

Eva raised her head abruptly. "No, I've told you before, you can't tell Ryker. Harper is a powerful man. You know that, Avery. He can destroy my family. They'll be left with nothing. I have to do something else. If I could afford my own restaurant or something that would help me generate my own money then I could leave him, and I could take care of my family for myself. I wouldn't have to depend on him."

"What about Quentin? I bet he'll help you. I mean, at least point you in the right direction. The man has two restaurants, two highly lucrative restaurants at that. You can talk to him without telling him anything about you and Harper."

Eva shook her head and wiped her tears with the back of her hand. "No, I can't do that. Harper is no fool. He'll find out what's going on and I can't let that happen. I just can't. And anyway, I don't trust Quentin either. He might be one of Harper's buddies for all I know. And since Harper made me stop working at the rescue shelter, I haven't talked to Quentin." Eva didn't tell Avery about Quentin's text. She didn't think that was important. What was important was she didn't work with Quentin and he was not someone she needed to turn to anyway.

Avery got up from the sofa and walked over to a nearby table that had a box of tissue on it. Picking up the box, she returned and sat down next to Eva, placing the box into Eva's hands.

Eva took a few tissues and began wiping her tear stained face.

"He made you stop working with Quentin? For God's sake, why? What's wrong with that man? And he gave away your babies? Please tell me he hasn't hit you again, has he, Eva? And tell me the truth."

Eva didn't answer. How could she tell Avery that it had become a regular thing for Harper to slap her around.

"Look at me."

Eva slowly looked up at Avery.

"Oh, my God. Please tell me he hasn't been physically abusing you. I thought after the time you told me he hit you that one time that was it. I should have known better. Once a man raises his hand to a woman even one time, he'll do it again."

Eva cried fresh tears. "It's my fault. I made Harper into the monster he is, Avery. I did it." Eva poked herself in the chest. "If I hadn't slept with his son. Oh, my God, I've messed up everything and I've put my family's well-being in jeopardy. My whole life is ruined."

"Listen to me. First of all, you did not make Harper the way he is. That's entirely on him. I don't care what you did; you don't deserve to be knocked around, Eva. And as for your life, it is not ruined. It's only ruined if you stay in this mess of a marriage with that fool. We're going to find a way to get you out of this." Avery felt such pity for her friend. To see her in such a fragile state of mind made her frightened for Eva. "You know what? I think I have an idea that might work."

"What is it?" Eva sniffled and wiped her nose.

"I know you don't want to tell the girls but before you say anything just hear me out. What if the three of us—me, Meesha, and Peyton invested in opening a restaurant? You may not have money on hand, but we do. And you know Peyton has more money than all of us put together. Anyway, we have the money and the means. We have Ryker and Derek who can help us with all the ins and outs of starting a business so we wouldn't have to worry about that. And you, well you can cook your behind off. You could be the executive chef. It can help you, Eva. It would be a win-win for all of us. It would give all four of us something adventurous to get involved in."

Eva shook her head. "I couldn't do that. It would never work.

"Now you listen to me. It *can* work. It *will* work. You have to trust somebody, Eva. And you can trust us. I know Peyton runs her mouth but at the end of the day, she speaks the truth, most of the time," Avery stopped and laughed and Eva cracked a smile. "Anyway, she's a loyal friend and once she finds out what you've been going through she's going to do whatever she can to help. Peyton is the type of person that will take care of your parents without skipping a beat if Harper tried to cut them off. You know that."

"But I wouldn't want her or anyone to do that."

"I know but I'm just saying. That's the kind of person Peyton is. She can get on my last nerve but one thing we know about her—she's genuine. And she's going to speak her mind in front of our faces, not behind our backs. As for Meesha, you know she'll be on board too. I mean, at least think about it and pray on it, okay?"

Eva's phone rang. She pulled it out of her purse when she heard Harper's ringtone.

Avery watched as Eva answered the call, looking like a sick puppy dog. "I'll be there on time," she said into the phone. "Yes, I hear you. No, I didn't get a new outfit. I don't need anything new anyway. I have so many clothes in my closet with tags still on them. I'll find something appropriate."

When the call ended, Avery shook her head. At that moment she despised Harper and everything he was doing to Eva.

"I better go. I need to get home and see what I can find to wear." Eva rose from the sofa and grabbed her purse.

Avery stood too. "I hate to see you like this."

"I'll be okay."

"No you won't because you aren't okay now. If that fool lays another hand on you, I swear, you need to call the police, Eva. He can seriously hurt you. Don't you understand that it doesn't get better once a man starts beating you? Please, listen to me."

"I *am* listening. It's just that I have to get a plan in place. I can't just walk away."

"Then promise me you'll think about what I said about letting me, Peyton, and Meesha help you. Please, Eva. Whatever you have to do. Just don't keep going through this alone."

Eva hugged Avery and Avery returned her hug with a deep, affectionate embrace of her own. When they pulled away, Avery walked her to the door.

"Ladies day out is Thursday. You missed the last one so promise me you'll be at this one."

"I'll try, but I can't promise I'll be there."

"Look, you know if at any time you need me, I'm just a phone call away. I don't care what time of day or night it is. If that man lays another hand on you, get out of that house. I wish you would leave already."

"I told you I can't, Avery. Not right now."

They hugged again.

Before she walked out of the door Eva turned and looked at Avery. "Please promise me you won't say a word to Ryker. Please, Avery."

"As much as I hate to promise you something like this, I won't say anything."

14

"Sometimes the heart sees what is invisible to the eye." H. Jackson Brown, Jr.

Peyton was over the top with excitement and expectation as she and Derek sat across from the fertility specialist. This was more than a dream come true; this was like she was living a whole new life. She couldn't thank God enough for all the doors he was opening for her and Derek. Their marriage was better than ever and their sex life—oh my God, it was like they were young teeny boppers with unlimited sexual energy. Now here they were in the doctor's office and Derek held tightly to her hand.

"Mr. Hudson, I'm glad you're here. I think this can be an exciting time for the both of you. Bringing a child, a wanted child, into the world is a remarkable thing. And in today's society and times, there are more chances to help couples like you to conceive."

"I appreciate that, Dr. Thomas. Could you tell me what the difference is in IVF and artificial insemination. I mean, of course I've done some research on my own ever since my wife and I talked, but going on line and hearing it straight from a professional are two different things."

"Yes, and you don't know how happy that makes me to hear you say that. I'm glad you understand the importance of getting reliable information from a specialist such as myself rather than relying on online sources which can be misconstrued and give you false information. But to answer your question, let's start with artificial insemination. Artificial insemination will involve inserting your sperm directly into your wife's cervix, fallopian tubes, or uterus. The most common method of artificial insemination is intrauterine insemination or IUI. That's what I plan to do if you all decide to move forward with this. With IUI I will place your sperm directly into her uterus. By doing that it helps the sperm get around any obstructions and makes the trip shorter for the sperm to travel. This hopefully results in her becoming pregnant in a normal fashion. I recommend this procedure first for you and your wife."

Derek nodded to show his understanding of what Dr. Thomas explained, while squeezing Peyton's hand. At one time during the visit, Derek leaned over and kissed his wife on the cheek. His affection toward Peyton almost made her cry with happiness, but she held back her tears.

"If after several attempts your wife doesn't become pregnant we will move forward with in vitro. In vitro or IVG involves combining the eggs and sperm outside of the body. Your wife's eggs and your sperm are mixed together in a culture dish for fertilization to take place. Once the embryo or embryos form, they will be surgically placed inside Mrs. Hudson's uterus."

"Will it be painful for my wife?"

"Whenever you undergo a medical procedure there is always the risk of experiencing some pain. Some more than others. But I will do my best to keep her as comfortable as possible if it comes to me having to perform IVF."

"Which is better, doctor? IVF or uh, I...U. I?"

"It can take several IVF cycles before your wife gets pregnant. The success of IVF depends on age, health status, and your own health and virility, Mr. Hudson, being her husband. With artificial insemination there is around a two to five percent chance for patients over forty years of age." The doctor briefly looked at Peyton's chart and then looked back up at Peyton and Derek. "Mrs. Hudson will be forty in a few months so you should have some idea of what percentages we're looking at. However, I would like to proceed with IUI first and if we aren't successful we can go with IVF. But, if the two of you insist and you want to bypass IUI and go directly with IVF then it's your decision to make.

"And the risks? Will she be safe?"

"Again, there are always risks associated with undergoing medical procedures. As for IVF, some women experience occasional bleeding and nausea after the procedure."

After their lengthy discussion, Derek looked at Peyton, smiled and then kissed her on the cheek before focusing his attention back toward the doctor. "I appreciate you taking the time to address my concerns, Dr. Thomas. If my wife is ready, then I say let's do this."

This time Peyton reached over and hugged Derek. This was a day she would never ever forget. If God continued to show her favor, she could possibly be holding her and Derek's child in her arms in less than a year.

Ω

On their drive home Peyton and Derek talked about the things Dr. Thomas told them.

"Do you want to try artificial insemination like Dr. Thomas recommended or go straight for in vitro?" Derek used his free hand to clasp hers while he drove.

"I don't know. I think I'm leaning more toward IVF. I mean, think about it. If I could get pregnant by insemination it seems to me I would have been pregnant already. All artificial insemination means is your sperm being placed into my uterus. So far that hasn't worked for us all these years we've been doing it the natural way. But I have to admit, the natural way is the fun way." Peyton's head fell back against the seat as she broke out in laughter.

Derek laughed too. "So, now that we've decided to move forward with having a kid, I think we can share the news with Liam."

Peyton smiled. "Yes, I'm so happy. I just hope he's as thrilled about it as we are."

"I don't think he'll have any objections."

"I don't think he will either," Peyton agreed. "I just wish I had been sober a long time ago and we tried this. Part of me feels like I robbed him of having a brother or sister, you know."

"Don't look back, Peyton," Derek consoled her as he rubbed her hand. "All we have is today. I'm just grateful things are the way they are now. You're not drinking anymore. Our family is better for it, too."

"Yes, I know but—"

114

"No buts. Now, do you want to stop and get a bite to eat before we go home?"

"Uh, sure."

"Okay, wherever you want to go it's good with me."

"I love you, Derek."

"And I love you, Peyton. Always have, always will."

15

*"Sometimes being a friend means mastering the
art of timing. There is a time for silence. A time
to let go and allow people to hurl themselves
into their own destiny. And a time to prepare to
pick up the pieces when it's all over."*
Octavia Butler

The ladies met at Adverse City's Beach
Club. They dined outside under the airy
elegant white seaside pavilion along the scenic
stretch of private uncrowded beach. The view
was breathtaking, showcasing sugar white
sand and glistening waters.

Peyton remained in her giddy state as she
shared the news with the housewives about
her and Derek's decision to try in vitro.

"When is the procedure scheduled?" Meesha
asked.

"In a few days. I can't wait. Knowing Derek
and I can have a child together is a dream
come true. I just wish we had done it years
ago. That way Liam would have been able to
actually grow up with a brother or sister. Who
knows, maybe more than one."

"But it is what it is. No need to look back and wonder what could have been. God's timing is perfect," Meesha emphasized.

"Yea, I guess you're right. Derek sorta said the same thing."

"And you probably wouldn't have been ready to bring a kid in the world anyway," added Avery. "Now that you're sober it makes a huge difference. And I'm sure Liam will be happy either way."

"Have you all told him?" Eva spoke up, still nervous about the fact she was going to share with the housewives everything that had been going on in her life.

"Yes, we told him."

"And?" said Meesha.

"And he was excited just like me and Derek. He even told me he's happy about the change in our family since I stopped drinking. I feel so blessed. I feel like my life is taking on a new start."

"It is," Meesha said.

"Yea, but please do not start back drinking, for Christ's sake," Avery said.

"Oh, don't worry. I'm not going to do anything to ruin my life and the life of my family ever again."

The ladies became quiet for a few minutes while they enjoyed their delectable food.

"Eva needs us," Avery blurted after she took a swallow of her beverage.

The ladies stopped eating and drinking, looking at Eva.

"What's going on?" Peyton was the first to ask.

"I...nothing. I'm good."

"Come on now, Eva. You're among friends. It's time to stop keeping secrets." Avery reached over and patted Eva's shoulder. "Eva's being abused physically and verbally."

"Huh?" Meesha said almost choking on the forkful of vegetables she'd just put in her mouth.

"I knew it. I told you Harper was going upside that head." Peyton spewed and pointed at Eva. *God, it had to have been them I saw that day. I can't believe it though.*

Eva burst into tears and immediately jumped up from the table and dashed off.

"What is wrong with you?" Meesha admonished while Avery rolled her eyes and got up from the table to go after Eva.

"What?" Peyton replied, acting as if she had no clue what she'd done.

"It's not a joke, Peyton. If Harper is doing what Avery just accused him of doing, abusing Eva, how could you make fun of that?"

118

"I wasn't making fun of anything? I was serious. All I said was I knew he was going upside her head. What's so wrong with that?"

"You can be so unnerving, so insensitive at times." Meesha took a bite of her food and a swallow of her beverage while Peyton shook her head and did the same.

"Okay, well, when she comes back I'll apologize. Geez."

Ω

Eva and Avery walked along the private stretch of beach.

"I knew this was a bad idea. I tried to tell you that."

"Eva, come on. You know Peyton. Her mouth has no filter, but she really doesn't mean any harm. You and I both know that she'll do whatever she can for her friends. I'm sure she didn't mean it the way it sounded."

"It's not Peyton. I know how she is. But I just can't do it. No one can help me. I'm going to go home. This was all a huge mistake. Coming here, thinking that you, Avery and Peyton would be the answer to my problems. I've been thinking."

"Thinking? Thinking about what?"

"About going back—to Bolivia."

119

Avery stopped walking and looked at her friend. "You can't be serious? What will going back to Bolivia solve?"

"I don't know what else to do. Maybe I can open up a small café or restaurant there. Maybe I can make enough to keep helping my family. I'm sure Harper would be glad to have me out of his life anyway. All I know is I can't stay with him anymore. I can't take another beating, another unkind word from him. I just can't do it. I can't be under his control anymore, Avery." Eva broke down and started crying again.

Avery wrapped her arms around her. Neither of them seemed to notice Meesha and Peyton walking up.

"What's going on?" Meesha asked as she and Peyton approached Eva and Avery.

Eva looked up and used her hand to wipe away her tears.

"Look, I'm sorry, Eva. I didn't mean any harm," Peyton apologized.

"I know you didn't, and it wasn't what you said. I've just been under a lot of stress."

"If Harper is abusing you, you need to get out of there," Peyton said. She walked up and gathered Eva into her arms and hugged her. "You don't deserve to be mistreated. No one does. We're here for you. I'm sorry if I sounded so insensitive. I didn't mean it. I really didn't. No way would I ever condone someone being abused. Please just get out while you can, Eva."

"Peyton's right. You've got to get out of there," Meesha agreed.

"That's what she was going to talk to us about," Avery interjected. "She needs our help. More importantly, she needs our monetary help. And it's not like a hand out."

"What do you need?" Peyton asked. "Anything you need, I've got you."

"Me too," said Meesha. "Just tell us what you need us to do. We've got you."

The housewives surrounded Eva in a tight circle, holding her and assuring her everything would be all right.

16

"There are some people in life that make you laugh a little louder, smile a little bigger, and live just a little bit better." Unknown

Eva took a chance and went to the rescue shelter to talk to Quentin. Avery went along with her for support just in case Eva wanted to renege on the plans she and the housewives had made.

Walking into the store, Eva sensed a flood of ease wash over her. She loved working at the shelter, loved the animals, the atmosphere, the whole environment. It was important work to her, not to mention the lucrative salary Quentin paid her. She had saved most of it by opening an account at Adverse City Credit Union. Initially, she thought about opening an account at Adverse City Bank but had second thoughts. She didn't want to take the chance of Harper discovering she had the account, plus Derek being bank president, added to her uncertainty. It wasn't that she didn't trust Derek; she had to follow her instincts, and her instincts said she should place her money somewhere else.

A man about her age approached her and Eva. "Welcome to Scooby Doo's, ladies. How may I help you?" His smile was welcoming and his voice pleasant and courteous.

Eva surmised he was a new employee or intern; she'd never seen him before. "Hi, I...is Quentin here today?"

The man looked at her curiously. "Uh, no, I'm sorry, Mr. Winters is not here today. But I can help you. What is it you're looking for?"

"She used to work here and she's a personal friend of Quentin's," Avery stepped up and said, not giving Eva a chance to reply.

"Oh, I see."

"When will he be back?" Eva asked.

"The first of next month. He's out of the country."

"Oh, is that right?" Avery said and turned to look at Eva. "Well, thanks." Avery looped her arm into Eva's and led her toward the door.

"Are you sure there's nothing I can help you with?" the man offered again as he extended a hand out toward the women.

"No, thanks," Avery said and they exited the store.

"Out of the country? Maybe he went to Paris. That's where his restaurant is. He usually goes over there every couple of months."

123

"And you haven't heard from him? I mean, you worked for the man and you said the two of you were friends. Seems like he would have contacted you or let you know he was going to be out of the country."

"I, well, he did call and text me a few times, but he didn't say he was out of the country. And, well, to be honest, I didn't answer him anyway."

"What? Why?" Avery asked as they walked to the parking lot.

"I don't know. I guess with Harper forcing me to quit after he found out I was working for Quentin, it freaked me out. I don't know who to trust, Avery. I got all paranoid, thinking Quentin could be one of Harper's spies or something. I know it sounds crazy, but it's true."

They arrived at Avery's car and got inside. Sitting on the parking lot, they continued to chat.

"Look, I understand, but for some reason I don't think Quentin is a man who can be bought. Granted, I don't know much about him, but my spirit tells me you don't have to worry about him betraying you. And his grandmother, Emma Winters, is a force to be reckoned with too. I know she's not about that kind of business."

"But she adores Harper so I don't know who will or won't do what."

"She loves herself some Derek Hudson too, so you said that to say what?"

Eva shrugged. "I don't know. I'm so confused, nervous, scared."

"I hope you aren't still thinking about going back to Bolivia."

"Avery, all I know is I have to do something. I have to make something happen."

"Didn't we say we're going to help you open a restaurant? Peyton and Meesha are already on it, and so am I. And if you think about it, we don't need Quentin. There are plenty of people who will be willing to give us some guidance about opening a spot. We're going to meet Peyton and Meesha now to check out some places, so get going back to Bolivia out of your mind. As for Harper, if he lays another hand on you, you need to get the heck outta there. To be honest with you, I wish you would leave him right now. Don't wait on him to raise a hand to you again. That or you need to get yourself some protection."

Eva jerked and looked over at Avery. "What? Protection? What kind of protection?"

"Like a gun." Avery looked back, noticing the funny look that came over Eva's face. "What's wrong with you?"

"Nothing. I just can't believe you would even suggest that I get a gun. How can you think something like that?"

"Think something like what? All I'm saying is you're no match against a man like Harper. Hell, you're no match against any man that's beating the crap outta you unless you have something to fight him back with. All I'm saying is you need to get a gun, take some lessons on how to handle and use it, and if that fool steps to you crazy again, shoot him in the foot as my mother used to say she'd do to us if we ever crossed her." Avery laughed a little and Eva grinned. "If you don't want to do that maybe take some self-defense classes."

"I guess. I'll think about it." She didn't tell Avery she was almost one step ahead of her and that she'd visited a gun shop. But hearing Avery say what she said made her feel better. Maybe she wasn't evil after all like she'd convinced herself she was. Avery was right to a certain extent, she needed to be able to defend herself from Harper's attacks which were getting worse and more frequent. It took very little to set him off these days. That made it more crucial and necessary for her to become financially independent or she would definitely have to return to Bolivia for her own safety. Unless Harper followed her there. At this point,

Eva felt helpless and hopeless. No matter where she ran she feared Harper would find her. *God help me.*

"Have you heard anything I've said?"

"Yes, I'm listening," Eva said, escaping from her thoughts and returning to the conversation at hand.

"Don't you think you need to leave him?"

"I want to, but you don't understand. Harper is a powerful and dangerous man. If I leave him, there's no telling what he might do. And I know he'd find me."

"You can get a protective order against him."

"But I've never even called the police on the man. I've hidden all of my bruises and the ones that are still visible have almost faded away. I mean, there's no record of abuse. He'll just deny it so no, I don't think a protection order will work. Plus, I've read and heard that even if a person has a protective order if someone wants to bring harm to you they can and will do it. By the time the police arrive, that's if you have time to call the police for help, the person would have done what he wanted to do and be gone."

Avery shook her head as she drove off the parking lot. "My God, Eva. Something has to be done. I know you don't want me to talk to

127

Ryker, but please consider talking to someone. We can find an attorney in Miami if that will make you feel better. Or we can go farther away than that. But please, just promise me you'll talk to someone. You need legal advice. Real bad and real soon."

Sadly, Eva had to agree. "I hadn't thought of finding someone in another city. Maybe I will try that. Will you go with me?"

"You know I will."

Ω

The housewives met with a realtor who took them to tour several spots throughout Adverse City and Miami that would make good locations for a restaurant. Three of the places she showed them were former restaurant spots and two others were vacant buildings. The last two she showed them were restaurants in Miami that were still open but up for sale. The last one was a former restaurant that piqued Eva and the other housewives' interest.

Eva talked to the owner of the Spanish restaurant and learned he and his family would be returning to Spain and opening up a restaurant there. They wanted to sell their restaurant as quickly as possible.

"I like this space," Peyton said as they walked through the spacious restaurant.

"And there's plenty of foot traffic and customers so that's a good thing," Meesha said as she looked at the people. "This is lunch time so this lets you know how busy it's going to be."

Eva ventured over to where she saw a menu holder and picked up one of the menus and studied it.

"What do you think?" Peyton asked and positioned herself next to Eva.

"It's the typical Mexican cuisine, but I would make some drastic changes to it and also raise the standards here to make this more of a fine dining establishment, perhaps without the fine dining costs that usually comes with that."

"I think your Bolivian dishes would do well," Avery added as she looked over Eva's shoulder at the menu as did Meesha.

"No matter how you change the menu, the food is going to be delish," said Meesha.

"So what you're saying is you'll buy him out and keep the name and menu?"

"No, I was just looking at the menu. I'm going to change the name, but I'll keep some of the items he has on the menu. I'll put my own twist on it and then of course my signature Bolivian dishes like you all suggested." Eva found herself growing excited at the thought that because of her friends her dream might become a reality.

"Are you going to tell Harper?" Peyton asked.

"I don't see how I can avoid it."

"I wouldn't tell him you own it."

"That wouldn't be a lie because I don't own it—the three of you do or you will own it."

"That's not true. You're one of the owners too. We just won't broadcast it," said Avery in a reassuring voice.

Meesha side hugged Eva, "Yeah, Avery's right. We may be providing the upfront money, but your name is going on the deed of this place right beside ours. Once you start raking in the dollars you'll be able to buy us out. That is, if that's what you want to do."

"No, I wouldn't dare think of buying you out. I love the fact we all have a stake in this place."

"Sounds like you're leaning more toward this one rather than the other two contenders," Peyton said.

"What do you think?" Eva looked at her friends.

"I like it. The location is superb," Meesha said.

"A built in customer base," Peyton added.

"Doesn't look like it requires much updating," said Avery.

"Well, I do want to do some updating and remodeling," Eva said.

"Of course, that goes without saying, but it looks like it wouldn't take a whole lot to make this place grand," Meesha said.

Eva laid a hand over her heart and inhaled before slowly exhaling and looking around.

"What is it?" asked Meesha.

"This is all so....so unreal. Imagine me, a poor girl from Bolivia, having my own restaurant." Tears trickled from her eyes and down her cheeks.

"Come on now, no boo hooing. Let's sit down, eat lunch, and decide if this is the spot."

"Ladies," the realtor walked up, "what do you think of this place?"

"We love it," exclaimed Eva.

"Yes, this might be the spot," Peyton agreed.

"Well, let me know if you want to see some other places before you make a decision."

"I think we're done. At least for now," Avery told the realtor.

"We're going to stay and have lunch. You're welcome to join us," Meesha offered.

The realtor raised a hand. "No, but thank you. Just give me a call, Peyton, and let me know what you ladies decide. I'm at your beck and call."

"Thanks, Kateena," Peyton said.

"Bye now." She turned and walked away and out of the door.

"Are we ready to get our eat on, ladies?" Peyton laughed, grabbed Eva's hand, and they walked toward the hostess to be seated.

"I'm famished," Avery said, patting her belly.

"I second or third that," Meesha said and joined in on the laughter.

At this moment, Eva couldn't be happier. As she followed along with her friends, a sense of exhilaration filled her spirit. Maybe she hadn't ruined her life after all. To have friends like she'd found in Avery, Meesha, and Peyton was priceless. They were like family.

The ladies ate and compared the potential locations for their restaurant.

"The one negative, if that's what you'd call it, about this location is it's here in Miami and not Adverse City."

"I was thinking about that," Eva said. "That's about a forty-five minute commute we'd have to make."

"Uh, excuse me," said Peyton, "a forty-five minute commute you'd have to make every day. You're the one who'll be running the place and who would be the executive chef."

"True," said Meesha.

"For the price and this location, I don't see the commute being problem. Plus, it'll give you a reason to get a place of your own in Miami."

"Now, that's a good idea," agreed Peyton. "You need that. You'll be away from Harper and you'd have some peace. He wouldn't have to know about it. Not just yet."

Eva nodded as if she was in agreement and considering everything the ladies were sharing.

"The present owners have already converted the upper portion of the restaurant into a living space. You could use that if you needed to as a place to lay your head," said Peyton.

"That's true, but I was thinking we'd turn the upper space into a private dining area. You know for something like VIP clientele. They could get special perks and things as a VIP."

"I like that idea," said Meesha. "Girl, you got your head on right." Meesha laughed and the others joined in. "So, what do you think about the forty-five minute commute?"

"I don't see it as much of a problem. Like Peyton said, maybe I could find a small apartment or house here in Miami. But until then, I'm sure I'd get used to the commute in no time."

"Sounds like we've made a decision. Am I right, ladies?" asked Peyton.

"I say yes to making an offer," said Meesha.

"It's a yes for me, too," said Avery.

"And you, Eva?" asked Peyton.

Eva looked at each of them, smiled, raised her glass and said, "To Eva and Friends Bolivian Cuisine."

The ladies raised their glasses to meet Eva's. "To Eva and Friends Bolivian Cuisine."

"Definitely have to revisit that name," laughed Avery.

17

"In the arithmetic of love, one plus one equals everything, and two minus one equals nothing."
Mignon McLaughlin

For the past seven weeks, Derek had been administering a daily injection of medication to Peyton's abdomen, thigh, and sometimes her upper arm to stimulate her ovaries to form multiple eggs.

"Nervous?"

"I am," replied Peyton as she and Derek got dressed. "I thought I was nervous when Dr. Thomas did the egg retrieval, but I'm more nervous today than I was then."

Derek finished buttoning his shirt and then walked up to his wife and kissed her tenderly. "Everything will be fine. You've been a champ."

Peyton smiled. "Thanks, babe. I'm praying this works."

"Well, so far so good. I know this whole thing has been physically and emotionally taxing, but I can't tell you how much your being willing to do this means to me. I love you so much, Peyton."

"I love you too, Derek and I want to give you a child so badly." Peyton had to keep herself from crying.

"You've already made me happy. You and Liam are the center of my life." He embraced her and held her next to his chest.

Ω

Dr. Thomas went back through the steps she was going to take to make sure Peyton and Derek understood what was about to take place. "Before I start the procedure take this valium. It'll help relax your uterus."

Peyton took the valium and lay back on the hospital bed. Within minutes she felt the relaxing effects of the tiny pill.

"I'm going to place the embryos through your cervix and into your uterine cavity. After the procedure is done I want you to go home and remain in bed for the remainder of the day. Avoid any strenuous activities or exercise, and please abstain from sexual intercourse until we do a pregnancy test. I'm also going to prescribe a progesterone supplement. It prepares your uterine lining for attachment of the embryos. I want you to start taking the injections tomorrow. Do you have any questions so far?"

"No, I understand," Peyton answered and then looked at Derek.

"Clear as a whistle," said Derek.

"Okay, we're going to start," said Dr. Thomas.

The procedure went off without any problems and Peyton and Derek returned home. He treated her like she was a fine piece of expensive china.

Liam was sensitive to his mother's needs as well and asked her repeatedly if she needed anything. He was excited when his parents first shared the news about their decision to try to have another child. It would take the pressure off of him being the only kid and give him more freedom to do his own thing.

"In two weeks we'll know if it worked," Peyton told Derek as he sat on the side of their bed after having brought her a tray of food.

"Yep, but I have a feeling it's going to work on this first attempt. You watch what I tell you. When we go back to see Dr. Thomas you're going to be pregnant. Watch what I tell you."

"I sure hope your premonition is right."

"Hey, even if you don't get pregnant this go round, as long as you say you want to keep trying, we have more frozen embryos." He leaned in and kissed her again.

"I want to try until we can't try anymore."

Ω

Meesha, Avery, and Eva drove to Miami to the new restaurant. "I wish Peyton could have come with us," said Eva.

"At least she was able to go to the closing, and we wouldn't want her to miss today. She and Derek are at the final step of IVF," Avery remarked as she drove along the interstate.

"I'm so happy for her and Derek. Carlton and I have been lifting them up in prayer," said Meesha from the back seat.

"That's good," said Avery.

"Avery?"

"Yes."

"Tell me something," said Meesha.

"What is it?"

"What's the real deal about you not coming to church like you used to?"

Avery focused even harder on the highway. She swallowed hard, changed lanes, and then answered. "I don't feel it right now. I'm all churched out."

"I think I know what you mean," Eva agreed, also knowing the real reason for Avery's decision. "But I was thinking for me it's because of Harper. I feel like such a fake. You know, sitting beside him every Sunday knowing he just beat me the night before, and sometimes the same morning before we leave for church. Sometimes I even feel like God has turned his back on me."

"Oh, Eva, God will never turn his back on you," Meesha replied. "He's not that kind of God. You have to know that everything works out for your good if you love Him. And as for you, Avery. I have no idea what's going on with you. You know how good God has been to you. Ryker and the children are there just about every Sunday. I would think you would want to come to church with your family. You are so blessed."

"I know all of that, Meesha, but you just don't understand. I wish I could explain it, but I can't. Look, let's just change the subject."

Thank God the GPS lady gave her a reprieve from Meesha's interrogation.

In a little less than an hour after leaving Adverse City they turned on the street leading them closer to the restaurant. They passed several business establishments and hotels. The scenery was beautiful but it had nothing on the majesty and beauty of Adverse City.

"Hold up. Slow down," Meesha suddenly screamed.

"Girl, what's wrong with you?" Avery said as she pushed on the brakes, making the car come to a slow roll.

"That's Carlton's Bentley."

"Where?" asked Avery.

"Yeah, where?" asked Eva.

"Over there. At the Hilton Miami." She pointed toward the hotel parking lot. "Turn around, Avery. Please."

"Girl, Carlton is not the only man who drives a black Bentley."

"I'm telling you, that's Carlton's car."

Avery continued to drive until she could make a proper turn to go back to the hotel.

I know that dog isn't cheating on Meesha again. Lord, please don't let it be, Avery thought.

Oh my God, please don't let it be Carlton's car, Eva said in her mind.

Avery pulled up in the parking lot behind the Bentley. There was no mistaking it was Carlton's car. His signature tags said it all – PSTR P316.

"Okay, so it's his car. What does that mean?" asked Eva.

"It's probably nothing. I mean he could be meeting some of his pastor friends or something. It's just that he didn't tell me he was coming to Miami this afternoon."

Just as she suspected, Avery believed Carlton was up to no good. After all, he had invited her to meet him at this same hotel when they had an affair. *He could have at least chosen another spot to take his probably clueless side piece. Dummy.* Avery eyed Eva who was sitting next to her in the front seat. Both of them knew the sneaky adulterer Carlton could be.

If he *was* messing off on Meesha again, Avery prayed, though it would tear Meesha apart, she hoped he would be exposed for his cheating ways sooner rather than later. She just didn't want to be the one to do it. Carlton had shown her his evil side and she was not the one to approach him. She'd learned her lesson.

"Meesha, why not just call him? See where he is. That'll settle that."

Meesha relaxed against the back seat as Avery slowly moved past Carlton's car and found a parking space nearby.

"We can't sit here all afternoon. The building contractors will be at the restaurant in about an hour. I don't want to be late," Eva reminded Avery and Meesha.

"Okay, let's go. I'll talk to him later. Like you said, I'm sure it's no big deal. I don't expect him to tell me every move he makes anyway. I trust my husband." Meesha sounded like she was trying to convince herself more than her friends. "Come on, Eva's right, we don't need to be late. Let's go."

Avery maneuvered out of the parking space and drove off the hotel lot, exhaling and thanking God they avoided the drama of Carlton Porter—that is if he was in there with some other chick.

18

"Good friends help you find important things when you have lost them. Your smile, your hope, and your courage." Unknown

The meeting with the building contractors went well. All three housewives were pleased with the plans they'd made for the restaurant remodel. They texted images to Peyton to keep her in the loop.

"I hope Peyton's procedure went well," said Eva as the ladies enjoyed lunch.

"Have either of you heard from her?" asked Avery.

"I haven't," said Eva.

"Me neither, but she'll call us when she can. I'm so happy for her, Derek, and Liam," said Eva.

"Me too," Meesha said. "I pray she gets pregnant behind this."

"I think she is," added Avery but Eva remained quiet. "You ladies ready to head back to Adverse City?"

"Yep, I'm done. My food was delicious."

"I can't help but agree. This vegan food you suggested we try is a hit," said Avery.

"Why, thank you, Avery. I keep telling you all to give it a try. I must admit I haven't tried this particular vegan spot, but I'm glad it didn't disappoint. I'll have to make sure Carlton brings me back here again."

"Yeah, the food is wonderful." Eva put her fork down after eating her last bite. "This gives me an idea. I think I'll include several plant-based dishes on the menu, too."

"Hey, that's an excellent idea. It'll bring in an even larger clientele. I love it." Meesha's excitement resounded in her voice.

"Okay, it's a go. We're going to do it. I'll start looking for some recipes and practicing on preparing them at home. You ladies will be my taste testers." Eva laughed and so did the girls.

Eva, Avery and Meesha pushed back from the table and stood to leave.

"Back to Adverse City we go, unless you ladies want to do a little retail therapy." Avery giggled as she drove.

Ω

The ladies took the same route, meaning they would pass back by the Miami Hilton. As they got closer to the hotel, Meesha called Carlton. She told herself it wasn't to check up on him, but she was going to let him know she saw his car at the hotel. He would tell her that he had a meeting and that would be that on that.

Carlton didn't answer. She thought nothing of it, but she followed up with a text telling him to call when he got some free time. She didn't know why she didn't tell him she was in the vicinity of where she'd seen his car, but she didn't.

Approaching the hotel, all three ladies glanced at the parking lot. Carlton's car remained parked. At least three and a half hours had passed since they passed the first time.

"Pastor Porter is having a long meeting," said Avery, not meaning to sound sarcastic, but she did.

"*Oh dios mío!*" Eva exclaimed suddenly.

Avery stopped as the traffic light changed from yellow to red. "What is wrong with you? What did you just say?"

Eva immediately regretted having screamed. Meesha followed Eva's eyes.

Avery looked around too. They all zeroed in on Carlton's Bentley as two people approached it, walking hand-in-hand, laughing in each other's faces. The man and woman shared a light kiss before he opened the passenger door and allowed her to get inside.

Meesha, Avery, and Eva sat frozen until the driver behind Avery blared its horn, signaling the traffic light had changed to green.

Avery didn't move. It took several more blows by the driver behind her before she came back to reality and began driving.

"Pull up somewhere—anywhere," Meesha ordered, "and park so we can see."

Avery followed Meesha's instructions and parked across from the hotel at a restaurant.

"Did I see what I just think I saw?" Avery asked.

Meesha broke down in tears. "I can't believe it. Was that Carlton? Maybe it wasn't Carlton. It *was* Carlton. Carlton and...and his sister-in-law."

Eva looked in the back seat at Meesha. Her heart filled with sorrow for her.

"No, you're wrong, Meesha. That wasn't Carlton. It was somebody who looked like Carlton. Maybe his brother, Martin. Yeah, his brother must have borrowed Carlton's car," Avery said, knowing darn well their eyes hadn't fooled them.

The Bentley did not move. It was harder to see but the three of them watched the car from where they were parked. Meesha strained but she could still clearly see the two heads of the occupants. It looked like they were in conversation.

Avery watched too. Her hand flew up and over her mouth when she saw the couple lean into each other and start kissing again.

Eva bowed her head. She didn't want to see them making out. It hurt her too much. Poor Meesha.

"Is that? Was that? That's Carlton and that's Evelyn, Martin's wife with him." Meesha acknowledged in a state of denial. Without warning, she opened the door and jumped out of Avery's car.

"Meesha, wait. What are you doing?"

"What does it look like I'm doing?" she yelled as she headed for the street.

Avery and Eva jumped out of the car too, chasing behind her. Avery grabbed her.

"Meesha, don't do this. Stop and think. You need to be sure that's Carlton. It has to be his brother. It just has to be."

"I'm telling you, that's Carlton and that's his skank sister-in-law! I can't believe this. Oh, God!" Meesha cried and Avery and Eva pulled her back toward the car.

"Listen to me. You are *not* going over there. Get back in the car and let's just wait and see what they're about to do. If that really is

Carlton, you need to devise a plan against his sneaky behind instead of running up on him."

Eva nodded in agreement, knowing how violent Carlton could be after Avery told her how he treated her. "Avery's right. You don't need to go over there. Stop and think, Meesha. Please."

Meesha allowed them to lead her back to the car. Back inside Avery's car, Avery began taking pictures with her phone camera, making sure to zoom in as close as possible so she could capture a good image.

"I think I'm going to go to the hotel lot and see if I can park a little closer without them detecting me."

"I don't think he'll notice you anyway. He's too busy making out with that slut," Meesha said, still crying.

Avery drove across the street and parked a few cars across from where Carlton's Bentley was parked. She was thankful she drove her white Lexus because it did not stand out like Carlton's car. It blended right in with all the other cars parked on the lot.

Moments after she parked, and while the ladies continued watching, Meesha completely broke down when she saw Carlton open his door and get out of the car again. He walked around the front of the Bentley like he had no care in the world, opened the passenger door, and Evelyn climbed out. They embraced again, acting like newlyweds who couldn't keep their hands off each other. Carlton kissed her, and rested a hand on her behind as they headed *back* inside the hotel.

Avery and Eva took picture after picture of the couple. *That low down dirty dog. I thought I sunk to an all-time low when I slept with that devil, and I should have known better. Thank you God for saving me from the likes of Carlton Porter. And to think I wanted and thought RJ was his kid. Lord, have mercy on Meesha. She doesn't deserve this.* Thought after thought rippled through Avery's head. This was so wrong, so very wrong.

The ladies remained outside until Carlton and Evelyn disappeared inside the hotel. After waiting for at least thirty minutes, Meesha was determined to confront him.

"I'm going in there."

"Meesha, do you honestly think they're going to give you Carlton's room number if he is in there?" reasoned Avery.

"It's worth a try."

"Meesha, don't do this," Eva begged.

Meesha didn't listen this time, forcing Avery and Eva to go along with her inside the hotel.

Putting on an act that could have given her an Oscar, Meesha said politely to the young lady at the front desk, "I have a reservation please."

"Yes, ma'am. Your name."

"It's in my husband's name—Carlton Porter." Meesha smiled a fake smile at the young girl as she began looking on the computer screen for Carlton Porter.

"I'm sorry, but I don't have a Carlton Porter registered at our hotel. Are you sure you made the reservation under your husband's name?" the giddy girl asked.

"Oh, well, my husband actually made the reservation. I could have sworn he said he made it under his name. Are you sure you aren't overlooking it? Or just try my name, Evelyn. Evelyn Porter."

The girl smiled. "Yes, ma'am." Her brows furrowed as she searched again. After a couple of minutes she started shaking her head, she looked up at Meesha, eyed Eva and Avery before saying, "There's not a reservation under that name either. I'm sorry. Is there another name you'd like me to try?"

"Yes, Martin. Martin Porter."

Looking somewhat frustrated, the young lady looked for the reservation and again repeated the same thing to Meesha—there was no one by that name.

"Are you having trouble?" A man with MANAGER on his name tag approached and asked the girl.

"I was trying to help her find a reservation but—"

"Forget it." Meesha threw up her hand.

"Come on, Meesha. Let's get out of here," Avery insisted and took hold of Meesha's forearm and led her away from the front desk.

Meesha looked around the elegant hotel lobby as if she was expecting to see Carlton and Evelyn. They were nowhere in sight.

Tears returned to her eyes as she walked out of the hotel with her friends. Her life had just taken a radical turn. *Oh what a tangled web we weave...*

19

"Don't go looking for trouble." Aesop

Eva filled her every waking moment taking care of business for the grand opening of the restaurant that was to take place in the upcoming months. The renovations were well underway and she was more than elated.

Surprisingly, when she initially told Harper about the housewives opening a restaurant he didn't seem bothered but Eva knew his disinterest could change at the drop of a dime. At first, her decision was not to tell him, but she didn't want to take the chance of him finding out, especially when she and the other housewives were planning an elaborate grand opening. He was sure to find out and the last thing she wanted was to be bruised and battered at her own opening. The lesser of two evils, she decided, was to tell him.

"And you say you're not part of this restaurant thingamajig?"

"I told you I'm the executive chef. I can't believe my dream is coming true, Harper."

"As long as it doesn't interfere with the show and you running our household. The first sign I see that you're getting your priorities skewed then that's going to be it."

Eva didn't remark; she continued preparing a new dish she'd been working on.

"What part does Quentin Winters play in it? I'm sure those housewife friends of yours turned to him for some advice, huh?"

"Why would you say that?"

"I mean, be for real. The guy is a successful restaurant owner himself. And since you and he are chummy chummy, I'm sure you asked him for his input."

Harper sat at the island, holding the Adverse City General newspaper in one hand and a cup of black coffee in the other.

"Well, you're wrong. He has nothing to do with it. Ryker and Derek have been the biggest help. Ryker used his lawyer connections to make sure the ladies got the best legal assistance and Derek handled the financial side of it."

"I'm surprised you didn't put any money in it or ask me to invest in it." Harper eyed his wife suspiciously, waiting to see if there was any sign she was hiding something.

"I didn't ask you to invest because it's not like you and I are on the best of terms, Harper. Plus, you're already taking care of me and my parents. I'm satisfied being the executive chef.

153

I'll be able to make money of my own and gain some notoriety one way or the other. That means whether customers like my food or not I'm going to hear about it. Let's just hope it's on the positive side."

Eva continued mixing ingredients together.

"Well, I'm leaving. I'm not sure what time I'll be home but it'll be late."

Eva said nothing.

Harper set the coffee cup on the island, tucked the newspaper underneath his arm, got up, and walked over to the other side of the kitchen where Eva stood.

She didn't turn around or stop what she was doing until he grabbed her forearm and swished her around. It almost caused her to drop the mixing spoon she held in her hand.

"Harper!"

Harper disregarded her outburst and instead began kissing her hungrily while his hands traveled along her body, causing Eva to almost become physically ill.

There was a time his touch would have set her afire, and she would have wanted him to make love to her like there was no tomorrow. But that was no more. She was not in love with him anymore, and practically despised him. His touch sent shivers of ice through her veins but she knew better than to pull away or to act as if she wasn't enjoying his kiss. It may have taken her several beatings, but she'd finally gotten the picture. It was easier this way. All she needed was time. Time to make money from the restaurant. Time to make a name for herself. Time to have enough resources to get away from him.

"See you later."

"Sure," and she turned to resume preparing her dish. She breathed a welcomed sigh of relief when he left. Minutes later Marissa walked into the kitchen.

"Good morning, Senora Stenberg."

"Good morning, Marissa."

The two ladies exchanged conversation and Marissa watched as Eva placed the casserole into the oven.

"Are you okay?"

"I'm good, Marissa. I miss my babies, but other than that, I'm doing okay. My focus is on being successful with the menu for the restaurant. You've been a big help. And like I told you, I want you to be my sous chef. Are you still considering my offer? I've already talked to the housewives and they're in agreement of me bringing you on board."

"I will try. I must see if Dr. Stenberg approves, you know."

"Yes, I know. And I've mentioned it to him. So far he hasn't said no, but he hasn't said yes either. I figure as long as it doesn't interfere with what you do here then he should be okay with it."

"Maybe. Dr. Stenberg can ...well, I don't want to upset him," is all Marissa said and proceeded to clear away the dirty dishes and utensils Eva had used.

"No need to do that, Marissa. I'll clean up my own mess."

"I don't mind. I hope you do good at the restaurant."

"Thank you, Marissa." Eva turned and embraced Marissa. Marissa was the closest thing she had to a mother in the United States.

Her phone rang, bringing closure to their conversation and show of affection. Eva walked over to the island, looked at the screen and then answered it.

"Hello."

"Wow, I can't believe you actually answered. How are you?"

"I...I'm good, Quentin. How are you?" she looked over at Marissa who had a half smile on her face.

Eva walked out of the kitchen and into the all-season room located through a double door exit at the back of the kitchen.

"I'm better now that I hear your voice. I've been calling and texting you but it seemed like you dropped off the face of the earth. I didn't think when you quit the shelter you would write me off as well."

Eva slowly paced and looked around the room like she was expecting Harper to appear and catch her talking to his arch enemy. That is, if he really was Harper's enemy.

"That wasn't my intent. I...I've just had so much going on and—"

"Hey, no need to go into that now. I just wanted to let you know I'm back. Wanted to see if things had changed. You know, maybe you would be able to come back to the shelter."

"Back from where?"

"Oh, I didn't tell you? Of course, I didn't," Quentin paused. "Anyway, I've been out of the country. Had to make my usual visit to my restaurant. I also went to New York, so I just made it back last night."

"I hope everything went well," Eva said, still sounding cautious.

"It did. My grandmother told me about the restaurant. So you're going to be the executive chef. Congratulations are definitely in order."

His voice was magnetic, enticing, hypnotic, but Eva had to push the ripples forming in the pit of her belly aside. The rapid beat of her heart was almost out of her control. She inhaled deeply and then released it, hoping it would make the feelings she had for him dissipate.

"Thank you," she said humbly. "I'm really excited. The opportunity the housewives are giving me is more than I can ever imagine."

"You're going to do fine, and the restaurant is going to flourish. From what I've been told, it's in the perfect location in Miami. And anything you ladies need, I'll be more than happy to offer my assistance."

"Sure, thanks. Well, look, welcome back to Adverse City. I, uh, I have a lot to do so I better get back to it."

"How about a celebration?"

"A celebration?"

"Yes. After all, I missed your graduation and you getting a gig as executive chef is big time. And I want to give you your graduation gift. I brought you something back from Paris."

"You shouldn't have, Quentin."

"Well, I did, so what do you say we meet for lunch later today. I know you're busy but busy lady or not, you still have to take time out to eat."

Eva closed her eyes momentarily and envisioned seeing Quentin. She missed him more than she had expected she would. But having lunch with him was totally out of the question. She could just see Harper barging in on them and that would be a total disaster.

"Thank you, but I...I can't, Quentin. Look, I really have to go. Thanks for calling. Buh-bye." She quickly ended the call.

20

"The truly scary thing about undiscovered lies is that they have a greater capacity to diminish us than exposed ones. They erode our strength, our self-esteem, our very foundation."
Cheryl Hughes

Meesha braced herself for a showdown while waiting for Carlton to walk through the door. The nerve of him and Evelyn. How could he? How could she? How could he betray the trust they shared? The years they had vested in each other. Her mind twirled with a million and one thoughts. What was she going to do? Say?

Anger consumed her until she could no longer restrain herself. Walking over to her mirrored dresser she picked up the music box gifted to her by her sister when she was a teenager. Picking it up, she hit it repeatedly against the mirror. With little effort the mirror cracked. With a swoop of her hand she raked everything on the dresser and onto the floor. Her tirade continued with her destroying everything in her path like a hurricane.

"What are you doing?" Carlton rushed in, grabbed her arm and stopped her."

"Get away from me! Don't you touch me! Don't ever touch me again! You lying, cheating dawg."

"What's wrong with you?" He held tightly to her wrists, restraining her but she bucked against him, fighting like a mad woman.

"How could you? How could you do me like this?"

Carlton was clueless. What could have happened to cause his wife to be in such a rage? Releasing one hand while Meesha continued pounding him with her free hand, Carlton managed to call Yulisa.

"Yulisa, where are you?"

"I'm at the park with Makena. I'll be here until it's time to pick up the boys. What's going on? What's all that noise? Is that Mrs. Porter?"

"Yes, she's acting like a mad woman. Do you know what's wrong with her?"

"No, Pastor Porter. She wasn't home when I left. She said she had to go to Miami to meet the building contractor about the restaurant she and her friends are opening."

Meesha continued screaming and howling like a roaring, mad lioness.

"Okay, thank you, Yulisa."

"Is she all right? She sounds like she's having a break down."

"I'll handle it. Thanks. I gotta go. Take care of the kids and call before you come home. I don't want the kids to see her like this."

"Yes, sir."

Meesha scratched and clawed at Carlton, drawing blood on his face, neck, and arms.

"Calm your behind down," he yelled, losing his composure as he threw aside his phone and wrestled her onto the bed.

Meesha kicked and clawed, one blow hitting him dead square in his genitals, sending Carlton reeling. He released her and grabbed hold of himself between his legs, bending over and screaming in agony.

"You're nothing but slime, a two-timing, good for nothing piece of crap, Carlton Porter." She jumped up off the bed and while he remained bent over she pounded him on his back and kicked him full force all over his body.

Using one hand he managed to knock her off her feet by grabbing hold of her ankle. Toppling her, he used both hands to pin her to the floor.

"I said stop it. I don't know what you're talking about, but if you don't calm down, I swear, Meesha, I'm going to call the police."

Meesha fought against him until she started hyperventilating. Her breath heavy. Tears like a river poured from her eyes.

"I saw you, Carlton. You can't lie your way out of this. Now it all makes sense," she said, still breathing heavily. She stopped fighting as Carlton slowly loosened his hold on her.

"Saw me where?" he asked as he still restrained her. "For God's sake, what are you talking about?"

"Turn me loose." She jerked.

Carlton did as she asked and released her but he didn't move from over her and Meesha remained on the floor.

"I saw you and...and her kissing and going into the hotel. What do you have to say about that, you dawg!"

Carlton tried to hide his surprise at hearing his wife's words, but he knew he was caught like a wild animal in a trap.

"Me and who? I don't know what you're talking about." He eased up off of his wife.

Meesha, still hyperventilating managed to get up off the floor. She pulled herself on to the bed but she didn't stop yelling and screaming.

"Don't you dare stand there and act like you don't know what I'm talking about. I have pictures and a video, Carlton. You and Evelyn," she cried. "I can't believe you would do me like

163

this. And Martin, how could you do this to your own brother, your own flesh and blood."

"Meesha, listen to me," he pleaded. "It's not like you think. There is nothing going on between me and Evelyn. For Christ sakes, what kind of man do you think I am that I would mess off with my brother's wife. Or that I would mess off period? Evelyn and I had a meeting earlier, that much is true, but it was nothing more than that. And you're talking about me kissing her—sure I may have kissed her in a nonsexual way though. Be for real, Meesha. I love you. There's no one but you. You're going off for nothing."

"I knew your wanna be slick behind would try to deny it, try to make me seem like I'm the one crazy or that I'm seeing things. Well, I saw things all right. And that was no platonic kiss. And to think I had that wench up in my house. How long have you been smashing her, Carlton? Tell me?" Meesha jumped up off the bed again and slapped Carlton so hard his head went to the side.

He rubbed his stinging face. "I don't know what you're talking about. You're not making any sense, Meesha."

He wanted to strike her back so badly but managed to maintain control. If she had been any other woman in the streets he would have floored her with the quickness. But this was the mother of his children, the first lady of Perfecting Your Faith. The bottom line was he had been caught. He had to remain calm so he could figure out how he would smooth this over. Yes he was in a world of trouble but with the help of the good sovereign Lord he would find a way to get out of it. If he didn't he could stand to lose everything. That was not going to happen.

"I want you out of this house--NOW, Carlton Porter! Nowww!"

"Look, I'll leave. I know you need time to cool off. Then we can sit down and talk this out. You'll see that you've blown what you think you saw totally out of proportion. Totally, Meesha. You just wait and see."

Carlton picked up his phone from off the floor and walked out of their bedroom, down the stairs, and went to the garage. He got inside his car where he sat for a few minutes before starting the engine, raising the garage door, and backing out of the driveway.

As soon as he pulled out onto the street he called Evelyn. "Brace yourself. All hell just broke loose. Meesha saw me and you at the hotel. Says she has pictures, too."

"Oh nooo, please tell me this is a prank."

"I wish I could. She went off like a wild woman, screaming, hitting me. It wasn't good. Not good at all. She told me to get out. I just wanted to warn you. I've got to think of a way to smooth this over. I'll hit you back when I can. In the meantime, you need to come up with something to tell Martin in case she calls you or him. I told her we were there for a meeting. At least I think I did. Anyway, she saw us kiss. I told her it was a platonic kiss, it meant nothing." Carlton rubbed his head back and forth as he drove nervously toward only God knew where."

"This can't be happening. Oh, God, Carlton, this is my worst nightmare. We've always been so careful. Lord, what if she calls Martin? I can't lose my family, Carlton. My kids. Oh, God, you have to fix this. You have to," Evelyn cried into the phone.

21

"Cheating on a good person is like throwing away a diamond and picking up a rock."
Unknown

Peyton was in disbelief when Avery and Eva called her on three-way. After asking how her procedure went they told her about Carlton and his sister-in-law.

"How could he be so stupid? If he was going to mess around you'd think he would've had sense enough not to be knocking off his brother's wife," Peyton said in Peyton fashion.

"I thought the same thing," Avery concurred.

"Me too, but then again I can't say a thing. Look at what I did and I'm still paying for my stupid decision," Eva said.

"You were vulnerable and horny," said Peyton. "Yeah, it was wrong to sleep with your husband's son, but dang, Harper wasn't throwing down in the bedroom and a young woman like you, well, anyway, that's a whole other subject. What did Meesha do? Have y'all heard from her since you dropped her off?"

"No," they both replied. "Did you get the pictures yet?"

"No...wait, hold up. I think they just came through." Peyton pulled her ear away from her iPhone, opened her text messages, and boom, there the images were as clear as the day outside. Two pictures of Carlton and Evelyn, and a video clip of them walking hand in hand and a picture clearly showing one of his hands placed firmly on her butt.

"OMG, I'd like to see how he's going to explain this," Peyton said.

"He can't. I mean if we hadn't seen them kissing and holding hands, he could have possibly convinced Meesha it was an innocent meeting or something, but girl, there's no denying something's going on between them."

"You know it," Peyton said while Eva remained a little less talkative, allowing Avery and Peyton to do most of the talking.

"Eva, you still there?" Peyton asked.

"Yes, I was just listening to you all. I feel so bad for Meesha. I'm still praying there's a simple explanation for what we saw. Meesha took him back one time but if it turns out he's cheating on her, I don't see her taking him back again."

"I agree. Their marriage might be over."

"And his sister-in-law's marriage too," Eva said.

"They say blood is thicker than water but in this case I don't know what Martin Porter will do to his brother. He's not going to be thinking about the man being his brother, preacher, or nothing. All he's going to be thinking about is beating the crap out of him," Peyton exclaimed.

"Babe, you're supposed to be resting," Derek said as he entered into his and Peyton's bedroom. His wife was laying in the bed but she was talking on the phone with whom he assumed was one of her girlfriends.

"Look, Avery and Eva, the hubby just walked in reminding me I'm supposed to be taking it easy so I guess it's my cue to hang up."

"Of course. You get some rest. I'm so glad the procedure went well," Avery told her.

"Me, too," said Eva.

"Thank y'all."

"We're praying that when you go back in two weeks you'll be good and pregnant," Avery said, laughing into the phone.

"I know right," Peyton agreed.

"Okay, we'll text you if we hear something. Bye girl."

"Bye, Avery. Talk to you later, Eva."

The ladies ended the call and Peyton relaxed her head back against the soft, thick pillow.

Derek walked up, sat down on the bed beside her, and kissed her. "I want you to do what the doctor tells you to do, sweetheart."

"I *am*, honey. That was Avery and Eva. They were just calling to see how the procedure went."

"Sounded like you all were talking about a lot more than that. I'm not trying to be hard on you, but I don't want to take any chances of you having complications. Take it easy, get your rest. I'll bring dinner up in a couple of hours. In the meantime, do you want something to snack on?"

"No, I'm good."

"You want some water, juice?"

"Baby, no, I'm good."

"I love you."

"I love you too, Derek. And I promise not to do anything that will jeopardize us having a baby."

"I know you won't." He kissed her again and stood up. "I'll be back later. Call me if you need anything."

"Hi, Mom," Liam appeared in the doorway.

"Hi, honey. How was practice?"

Derek exited the room.

"Good. How do you feel? Did everything go all right?"

"Yes, it did."

"When will I know if I'm going to have a kid brother or sister?" Liam walked all the way into the room, stopped at his mother's bed, and leaned down and kissed her on the side of her face.

"We have to go back to the doctor in two weeks. We'll find out then."

"Cool. You want anything? I'm going to take a shower and then do my homework."

"No, I'm fine. You go ahead and do your thing. I'll see you later this evening."

"Okay, Ma." Liam turned and walked out of the room then stopped and looked over his shoulder. "Do you want me to close your door?"

"Sure."

Peyton smiled. Her life couldn't have been better. She had her life back, her family back, and she and Derek's bond was stronger than ever. If she went back and Dr. Thomas told her she was pregnant, it would be the best news ever.

Her mind deflected on what Avery and Eva told her about Carlton. Poor Meesha. If Carlton was cheating on her, Peyton already knew Meesha would more than likely break. The woman called herself a woman of faith, a strong woman of God, but to Peyton, in some ways, Meesha was weak as water. A couple of years ago when Carlton was talking about he wanted a divorce but didn't give Meesha a real reason why, Peyton thought then Meesha was a fool. If Derek had stepped to her like Carlton did to Meesha, Peyton would have let him walk. Or would she? She thought about that again. She'd almost lost her family because of the whole Liam thing. Carlton and Breyonna were part of that mess, too. Peyton got her family back but at the same time Carlton was crying about he wanted to end his marriage. Thank God the man came to his senses. Peyton often wondered if his change of mind had anything to do with Breyonna's death while she was incarcerated.

"God, Meesha, I hope it's not what those pictures make it look like. For your sake," Peyton mouthed while picking up the remote from the side of her and powering on the television.

22

"Dear Karma, I have a list of people you missed." Unknown

Meesha curled up in her bed crying her eyes out for quite some time. Then something within said to her, *enough is enough.* Slowly, she sat up in bed, looked around the bed and on the nightstand until she saw her phone, and called Yulisa.

"Yulisa, can you take the kids out for dinner somewhere?"

"Yes, ma'am, I can. Are you okay?"

"Not really, but I *will* be. Just take care of the kids. And before you bring them home, give me a call. I need some alone time. If you can just tell them Mommy doesn't feel well and that I'm sleeping, it would be great. I can't let them see me upset."

"I understand. Is there anything else I can do? Do you want me to bring you something back to eat?"

"No, I'll be fine. I might go out for a while. Oh, and Carlton is not here. He probably won't be back tonight."

"Yes, Mrs. Porter."

"Thanks, Yulisa. You're a jewel."

"You're welcome. Call me back if you need me to bring you something."

Meesha remained in bed for a while longer and then suddenly got up, went to her closet, changed into a pair of jeans, a colorful t-shirt and a pair of sneakers. She pulled her curly natural up into a bun before getting her purse, keys and cell phone, and going downstairs and out to the garage.

She was not about to roll over and play dead. This time she was not going to let Carlton manipulate her into thinking she had been mistaken about what she saw.

Twenty minutes after leaving home, she turned onto Martin and Evelyn's street. If Carlton didn't give her the answers, she was going to get them on her own—one way or another.

She parked on the street, walked up to the Tudor style house, and rang the doorbell. Martin opened the door.

Looking surprised, he greeted his sister-in-law. "Hey there, Meesha."

"Hi, Martin. Look, I'm sorry to show up on your doorstep without calling, but I was in the neighborhood so I thought I'd stop by and talk to Evelyn. She and I have some things to go over."

"Oh, no problem. You know you're always welcome, Meesha." He stepped aside, extended his hand, and allowed her entrance. "Come on in, although Evelyn isn't here at the moment."

"Oh, okay. Guess I should have called." Meesha walked inside as Martin closed the door behind her.

Martin and Evelyn's kids appeared in the hallway. Both of them waved at Meesha. "Hey there."

"Hi, Aunt Meesha," each of them said.

"How are you, Martin? We hardly ever get a chance to really sit down and talk, but is everything okay?"

Martin's pleasant look turned serious. "Yes, sure. Why do you ask that?"

"Oh, no reason. I know you have a lot on your plate. Your involvement with the church, the academy, home life—you know, I'm sure it can feel a little much. And then trying to maintain a happy marriage and all."

"Uh, yeah, it can get a little stressful, but then again, I feel like it's what I've been called to do. At the end of the day I'm a blessed man. I'm doing what I love working in the ministry, involved with the youth, and as far as my family, I'm blessed beyond measure. Two healthy kids and a beautiful, loving devoted wife. What more can a rascal like me ask for?

175

God has shown favor over me and I'm grateful. I know you and Carlton not long ago had your problems, but thank God he came to his senses and realized what a gem he has in you, Meesha."

Meesha blushed while the other part of her became even more infuriated thinking about her and Carlton's marriage and what he'd subjected her to before with his talk about divorce and the mess with Breyonna, Liam, and Peyton. She forgave him only to find out now he more than likely was sleeping with Evelyn.

"Yes, but sometimes things aren't always as they seem, Martin."

"What do you mean? Is that brother of mine giving you a hard time? If he is, you let me know and I'll jack him up, set him straight." Martin laughed.

"Believe me, I know exactly how to deal with Carlton. Anyway, let me get out of here and head home."

"Are you sure? You can call Evelyn if you'd like—see how much longer she's going to be out. She went to hang out with some of her former co-workers."

Meesha didn't believe that *hanging out with co-workers* tale for one minute. Meesha threw up a hand. "No, it can wait, Martin. Believe me, what we have to talk about is not going away. I'll talk to her tomorrow. Anyway, bye, boys." She looked past Martin to see if the boys were still around but they said nothing.

"They're probably gone back in the media room. Before you came, we were watching Black Panther for the hundredth time."

"You go back to doing what you were doing. I'm sorry to disturb you."

"Sis-in-law, you're never a bother. I told you that." He walked Meesha the few steps back to the door, opened it, and before she walked out, he hugged her.

"See you later. Be safe out there."

"I will. Bye, Martin."

23

"Each player must accept the cards life deals. But once they are in hand, he or she alone must decide how to play the cards in order to win the game." Voltaire

"Meesha, you all right, girl?" Peyton texted. "Heard what happened."

Meesha was about to drive off from Martin and Evelyn's house when the text came through. She remained parked to answer Peyton's text.

"I'm good. OTW home. HRU? Glad the procedure went well."

"I'm good. Resting. Derek won't let me make a move on my own since the procedure. LOL

"Good for Derek. Well, take it easy. I'm driving. I'll call you tomorrow and fill you in on everything."

They exchanged several text messages without Meesha telling Peyton where she was and what she intended to do had Evelyn been at home. She was going to beat her down first and then tell Martin what had been going on between his wife and her husband. Evelyn didn't know how lucky she was not to be there.

But things weren't over—not by a long shot. She was going to confront her sooner or later.

"Ok. Love ya."

"Love you too, Peyton. TTYL."

Ending the text with Peyton she called Yulisa. "Hey, Yulisa. How is everything? Have you and the kids made it home?"

"Everything is good. I was about to call you. We're pulling up at the house now. Are you okay?"

"Not really, but I'll be fine. I'm not there but don't worry about me. I ran out for a minute to handle some business. Just take care of the kids. I'll be home soon. Let me know if Carlton is there."

"Yes, ma'am."

"And, Yulisa. I want to tell you that I don't mean to put you in the middle of what's going on between me and Carlton but I do want to let you know I put him out and I'm getting the locks changed. If he asks you anything, well, you don't know anything and that'll be the truth."

"Yes, but I'm sorry you and Mr. Porter are having problems. I thought when you and the boys came back from California everything was fine."

"Me too, Yulisa. Me too. But don't you worry. Everything is going to be fine. I'll be there soon."

Meesha's phone rang and her car dash showed it was Carlton. Driving up Adverse City Boulevard, she ignored his call and tuned into the music on the radio.

He called back to back at least three more times, and each time Meesha ignored it. Next, he started texting. Again she focused on the music. Turning it up so she couldn't hear the ding sound, she sang along with a song she liked by Kierra Sheard. *"He'll always come through for you...."*

Ω

Eva got out of the shower and as soon as she walked out of the bathroom, she knew it was going to be one of those nights when she saw Harper scrolling through her phone.

Dang, I forgot to delete the text thread from Quentin. Maybe he won't know the texts are from him since I don't have his real name in my phone. Please, don't let him act a fool tonight. I can't take it.

Before she could make it fully out of the bathroom, like a gazelle, Harper was up on her. The blow across her face knocked her to the floor, causing her towel to drop and she lay bare naked.

Holding the side of her face, she pleaded for him not to hit her again.

"You won't learn will you? Huh? You just won't listen to me. You want to go around being a two bit slut when I told you to stay away from Quentin Winters." He stomped her in her belly.

Eva screamed, "You're going to kill me, Harper. Please, stop. Oh, God make him stop!" Crawling backwards toward the bathroom, she looked quickly over her shoulder to see if there was anything, something, she could grab that would make him stop. There was nothing.

Harper continued his tirade, stomping and kicking her until blackness surrounded her like a shroud.

When she came to she was in her bed, lights out, and the house was eerily quiet. As her eyes focused in the pitch black, she saw she had on the gown she had laid out to put on when she got out of the shower. Had she put it on and somehow didn't remember? She tried to move but every move was filled with pain that ran through her entire body.

"Ahhh," she moaned. Trying to sit up, the pain pushed her back and she lay quietly as tears streamed.

A knock on her bedroom door startled her. *God, please don't let it be him again. Please.* God heard and answered her feeble prayer because she heard Marissa's concerned voice.

"Senora Eva, may I come inside?"

It hurt to talk but she answered weakly, "Yes, Marissa."

Marissa walked into the room, turned on the light, and used one hand to close the door behind her before she proceeded toward the bed with a tray of food and drink.

Sitting the tray on the night table next to the bed, Marissa quickly covered her mouth when she saw Eva. One of her eyes was literally swollen shut and her petite lips looked like she had an overdose of Botox injected into them. Her cheek was bruised and from what else Marissa could see, Eva's shoulders and arms were black and blue.

"Necesitas doctor," Marissa said, sitting next to Eva. Her heart ached for Eva. She had come to love her like she was Eva's mother instead of her employee.

Eva slowly shook her head. "No, I don't need a doctor, Marissa. Plus, he will beat me again if...if he finds out I saw a doctor. Too many people know him."

"You might have something broken."

"Where is he?" Eva whispered.

"He left for airport for the health...healthcare, uh summit."

Eva managed to exhale in relief. "Yes, in LA. Thank God. Are you sure he's gone?"

Marissa nodded. "Yes."

"How long have I been asleep?"

"It is noon."

"Noon? How can that be? It was only almost nine o'clock when I got out of the shower? Nine o'clock at night," Eva continued struggling to speak. The inside of her mouth hurt just as bad as the rest of her body.

"Yes, it is next day. Here, drink this hot turmeric tea. It will help."

"I've been asleep all night and half the morning?"

"Shhh." Marissa nodded. "No talk." She helped Eva sit up a little so she could take a sip of tea. After she took a few swallows, she forced Eva to eat some of the soup she'd made.

"You cannot take more beatings, Senora."

Eva cried. Marissa was right; she had to get away from Harper—that, or she had to make sure he would never be able to raise a hand against her ever again.

Marissa placed the bowl of soup back on the tray. Gently, she gathered Eva into her arms, lightly rubbed her hair, and spoke softly into her ear like she was trying to make certain no one heard what she was about to say. "God forgive me, but maybe I will do as you asked before, Senora— *mátalo.*"

24

*"Life is, at times, tough. And all we need to do is
to prove that we are tougher than it."*
Sanhita Baruah

Normally, on a typical weekday, Meesha
would be at Perfecting Your Faith Academy,
but she had more important matters to tend
to. She called Avery and Eva and asked if they
could come over. She needed their help.

Eva didn't answer her phone or text but
Avery did.

"Give me an hour," Avery told her. To think
that less than two years ago she couldn't stand
Meesha, was an understatement. My how time
changes things. How could she have ever
thought Carlton was the cat's meow. Instead
he was a vicious lying, sneaky, lion who
needed to be put down.

When Avery arrived, Meesha told her about
her plans. Avery laughed and readily agreed.
She was eager to help.

True to her word, Meesha contacted a
locksmith, changed every lock in the house,
had the security codes changed, and with
Avery and Yulisa's help packed almost every

stitch of clothing she could of Carlton's while the boys were at school.

After they were done, she contacted a local agency that accepted donations of clothing and other items. They were more than happy to send someone to pick up the clothing and some other personal items belonging to Carlton, including two Rolex timepieces, three diamond rings, several diamond necklaces and bracelets. She did leave him a suitcase full of clothing along with his personal Bibles and other church related items. She had those items picked up by a delivery service and delivered to Perfecting Your Faith.

This time she was done. She was not going to sit back and allow him or any other man to walk over her.

"Are you sure you want to go this far?" Avery asked as they watched the donation truck pull up into the circular drive.

"I've never been surer of anything in my life. I know what I saw; I have the proof in my phone. I don't want to hear his lies. He can save it."

"I just want you to be sure this is what you want to do. That's all. You have children with this man, you know. Y'all have history."

"He's history." Meesha and Avery stood in the door and watched as the two men from the agency approached.

"Mrs. Porter?" one of them said.

"Yes, I'm Mrs. Porter."

They displayed their badges and Meesha invited them inside so they could start gathering the items, and there was plenty to gather.

When they were finally done removing all of the items and left, Meesha and Avery went into the kitchen.

"Where are Makena and Yulisa?"

"Yulisa has her; it's time for her nap so I'm sure she's putting her down."

"Oh, I wanted to see her."

"You can check in on her before you leave."

"Okay, I will if she's not napping."

"Let's eat. Meesha opened the fridge. "What about we make ourselves a salad? I have all the fixings."

"Sounds divine."

They changed the subject while making the salad and talked about Makena and RJ and how fast they were growing.

When they were done, they sat at the dining room table and started eating.

Meesha said between taking a forkful of salad, "If you don't mind, I need another favor."

"Sure. Anything. What is it?"

"I need you to talk to Ryker. I want him to connect me to the best divorce attorney he knows."

"Are you serious, Meesha? You're going to divorce him?" Avery was about to put a bite of her salad into her mouth but stopped short.

Meesha looked at Avery. "Why are you acting like I'm the one who messed up the marriage?"

"That's not what I meant, Meesha. I'm just saying, you're angry, you're hurt, and you're acting out of your emotions."

"Maybe I am, but I won't accept a cheater, Avery. Anyway, I still can't get over the fact less than two years ago he was ready to throw our marriage away. He wanted a divorce and he didn't give me an explanation. He was ready to walk out on his children, his family, his marriage. Everything we've built. Now I know why. It was because of Evelyn."

Avery listened and started back eating. Taking a swallow of her bottled water, she slowly nodded in agreement. If only she could tell her just how much she knew Carlton Porter's true colors.

"I'll talk to Ryker this evening. "

"Thanks. Now that we've got that done, have you talked to Eva? I called and texted her to ask for her help too but she didn't answer. Her not answering our calls and texts is becoming a routine."

"Yeah, I know. I called her before I came over here, too. She didn't answer me either, but she did send a text. Said she wasn't feeling well. I kinda know what that means. Probably she and Harper got into it again. I'm going to stop by there and check on her when I leave here."

"Okay, let me know if she's okay."

"She needs to do like you—get rid of Harper, but you and I know she's too afraid of him cutting off her family's money. And they need that money. But to be honest, I believe the restaurant is going to take off for her, well for all of us. Not that we need the money like she does."

"Right, right." Meesha agreed. "Carlton is an adulterer, true enough, but he would never lay a hand on me. A man like Harper is dangerous and I'm afraid for Eva."

Again Avery thought about how little Meesha knew about her husband. Carlton almost choked her out without regard she was holding her baby boy. In Avery's eyes, Carlton Porter was just as vicious as Harper.

"But you know just like I do that most women caught up in abusive situations stay in it sometimes forever or until the worse happens, and they lose their life or are seriously hurt."

"Or until they kill their abuser," Avery added, taking the final bite of her salad.

"God, I pray she'll come to her senses before anything like that happens. She can't keep paying for the same mistake over and over again. Okay, she cheated, but she doesn't deserve to be physically or mentally abused. You know what I mean?"

Avery agreed. "I know right."

Meesha finished off her salad and water. "You want to go see if Makena is sleep?"

"Yes."

They went upstairs to Makena's room. Sure enough the little girl was asleep. Yulisa was in the bed across from Makena's crib fast asleep herself.

"Never mind. I don't want to wake either of them."

"Okay," Meesha whispered and the ladies turned and left.

"Call me later. You know Carlton is going to hit the roof when his stuff is delivered to the church and even more so when he finds the locks changed and his things gone."

"I know, but if he comes here trying to act a fool with me, I'll call the police on him in a heartbeat. I'm not playing, Avery. I'm done with Carlton Porter. And he hasn't seen nothing yet. I didn't tell you I paid a visit to Evelyn last night." The ladies stood in the foyer talking.

"You did what? What did she have to say?"

"She wasn't at home. Martin was."

"Please tell me you didn't tell Martin what you suspect."

"I couldn't do him like that, not yet. You know Martin told her I came over there so I'm sure she'll be calling or trying to show up here. She's going to hear from me one way or the other and she better hope I don't pull that weave out of her hair."

Avery laughed. "You know what?"

"What?"

"I don't like what Carlton or Evelyn did, but I do like this side of Meesha Porter I'm seeing. You...you're always so."

"Reserved, stuck up, shy acting, quiet, the church lady?"

"Uh, yea, you said it. I didn't, but yeah, all of the above."

Meesha and Avery laughed out loud again, embraced and Avery left.

Meesha closed the door, leaned against it, and slid down the length of the door. Resting on her buttocks on the floor with her knees gathered up, she inhaled, put her hands over her face, catching the tears as they gushed from her eyes.

25

"The scariest part of being part of a domestic abuse relationship is the idea that you cannot escape and you cannot get help, that feeling of being stuck." Kerry Washington

"Mrs. Mitchelson, I'm sorry but Mrs. Stenberg doesn't want any visitors. She's not feeling well. I can tell her you came by, but right now she's sleeping," Marissa explained when she answered the door and saw Avery standing on the other side.

"Is Harper here?"

"No, ma'am. Dr. Stenberg is out of town."

"Good. Look, Marissa, I know you're just doing what Eva asked you to do, but I'm going to see her whether she likes it or not. Something isn't right. I've called and texted her and she hasn't responded. Please just let me in." Avery gave Marissa a knowing look.

Marissa would never admit it but she was happy to see Avery Mitchelson. She was concerned about Eva. She remained in bed and it was now late afternoon going into the evening. She refused to eat anything other than the cup of soup from earlier.

Marissa stepped aside and invited Avery inside. "She's upstairs in her room."

"Thank you, Marissa."

"Of course."

Avery went upstairs and knocked lightly on Eva's bedroom door.

"Come in, Marissa."

Avery opened the door and walked inside. Eva was underneath the bed covers, hardly able to be seen.

Eva's eyes widened when she saw it was Avery and not Marissa. "What are you doing here? Did Marissa let you in? I told her I didn't want any company."

"Stop it, Eva. This is me you're talking to. I had to come check on you after I didn't hear from you. I know how crazy that husband of yours can get. Why do you have it so dark in here?"

Avery walked over and up to the custom made draperies. Before Eva could object she pulled them open and then looked down at Eva.

She gasped when she saw her best friend. "My God! Did he do this to you?"

Eva turned away as tears poured from her swollen bruised eyes.

Avery sat down next to Eva on the bed. She pulled the covers from her and saw more black and purple bruises on the upper portion of Eva's slender body.

Tears poured from Avery's eyes when she witnessed what Harper had done. "He's a monster, Eva. A terrible terrible monster. Come on, I'm going to get you out of here."

Eva looked at Avery. "No, I can't. I'm fine. Please go, Avery."

"Are you serious? You know darn well I'm not going to leave after seeing you like this. Have you seen a doctor?"

Eva cracked a half smile. "Doctor? Harper is a doctor."

"You know what I mean. Are any bones broken?" She reached out to touch Eva's face and Eva flinched as the mere touch caused her pain. She tried to sit up in the bed and with every movement she groaned.

Avery looked inside her black Hermes tote and removed her phone.

"What are you doing? Please don't call Harper. He can't know you're here. It'll only cause more trouble." Eva cried.

"Do you think I would call Harper? I should call the police, that's who I should call."

"No, don't," Eva tried to reach out to Avery and winced again.

"Meesha, I need you to come to Eva's—now." Next she called Peyton and told her the same thing."

"I'm on my way," Peyton said.

Avery got up and went to the bedroom door, opened it, and called for Marissa. "Marissa, Marissa."

Shortly after, Marissa appeared.

"Yes, Mrs. Mitchelson. Is everything all right?"

"You know it's not, Marissa."

Marissa looked past Avery and over at Eva who was half sitting up in the bed looking lost and forlorn.

"Mrs. Hudson and Mrs. Porter will be here. When they come please let them in."

Again, Marissa's eyes shifted from Avery and over to Eva who slowly nodded her approval. "It's...it's okay, Marissa."

"Yes, ma'am." Marissa turned to exit but then stopped and looked over shoulder. "Do you need anything? Something to eat? Drink?"

"No, I'm okay. Thank you, Marissa," she managed to say.

Ω

Peyton felt rested and ready to conquer the world. She was looking forward to the day she and Derek returned to see Dr. Thomas for the pregnancy results. For now, her concentration was on Eva. When Avery called, she sounded panicked. Her only thought was Harper had abused Eva again. Peyton didn't understand why Eva refused to leave him.

She turned on Eva's street, pulled up in her long driveway and as she came nearer, she saw Avery's car parked in front of the massive mansion. It wasn't as big as Peyton and Derek's but it was huge, nonetheless.

Parking her car, she got out and raced up to the door, ringing the doorbell repeatedly.

Marissa opened it and escorted her inside and up to Eva's bedroom where Meesha had arrived minutes before.

Marissa turned to leave as Peyton walked into the room, curiously looking at Avery, Meesha, and then Eva.

"Marissa, wait, don't leave. We need your help," Avery said to the nervous woman.

"Yes, Senora."

"Do you mind gathering some clothes and toiletries for Eva? We're taking her away from here."

"Si, of course."

Peyton walked up and stood in front of the bed. "Ahh, oh, my Lord." Both hands flew up and over her mouth. "What did he do to you?"

197

She rushed over to Eva's bedside and got an even closer look at the battered and bruised Eva.

"We're getting her to a doctor and she's not coming back to this house," barked Avery.

"I can't leave. He'll find me and it'll be even worse," Eva pleaded. "He'll kill me."

Ignoring Eva, Meesha spoke up. "You all don't know this, well, Avery does, but I put Carlton out. You're coming to my house," Meesha insisted. "You'll be safe there. I promise."

"Wait, you threw Carlton out? As in out of the house?" Peyton said, astonished at this revelation. "When?"

"Last night after we got back from Miami."

"Uh, are you serious?" She looked at Eva and then Avery.

"Yep, I'm afraid she's right. I wouldn't have believed had I not seen it with my own eyes."

"We told her everything," Avery said to Meesha.

Meesha nodded her approval. "Good, so you know why I did what I did."

"Did you confront him." I mean did he admit it?" Peyton asked.

"What's there to admit? He begged me to let him explain, but look at these. Does it look like I need anything explained? I think these say it all." She passed her phone over to Peyton after pulling up her photo gallery for her to see the pictures of him and Evelyn.

"For God's sake, how low can he go? All of this is insane. You, Carlton, Harper and Eva. Where's Harper? At the hospital?"

"No, he flew out of town last night. He'll be gone about a week," Eva said in a weak, barely audible voice.

"Come on, let's get you dressed." Avery went into Eva's closet and found her a pair of pants and a shirt and shoes.

Marissa was still gathering clothes and then left out of the closet and went into the bathroom to get some of Eva's personal items. A sense of relief filled her knowing Eva's friends were taking her away from this house of horrors. But what would Dr. Stenberg do when he returned and found her gone? That was something Marissa didn't want to think about.

"Here, put this on," Avery said and pulled the covers all the way back so Eva could sit on the side of the bed.

All three ladies gasped when they saw the rest of the bruises over her body.

Peyton was almost brought to tears as was Meesha but they said nothing. Instead they helped her sit up.

"I need to go to the bathroom," Eva said and began slowly walking bent over toward the bathroom. Each step she took there was a quick intake of breath as the pain raced through her body.

"I'll put your clothes in there," Avery said and walked ahead of Eva, placing the clothes in the bathroom so she could get dressed.

"Thank you."

"Call if you need us to help you," Avery offered.

Eva closed the door to the bathroom but within minutes the ladies heard a piercing scream.

Marissa was the first to get to the bathroom door and open it.

Eva continued screaming. "I'm bleeding."

"Bleeding?" said Peyton. "From where?"

Eva, sobbing, looked down in the toilet filled with blood.

26

"Friendship isn't about who you've known the longest; it's about who walked into your life, said, "I'm here for you and proved it." Everyday Blog

"What's happening to me?" Eva screamed.

"The ladies looked at all the blood in the toilet and pouring onto the tile floor when Eva managed to stand. Almost falling, Marissa halted the fall.

"I feel like I'm going to faint."

"We've got to get her cleaned up and dressed. We need to get her to the hospital," Meesha said, alarmed.

"Please don't take me to Adverse General. Harper will find out. Please."

"Don't worry about that. We've got this," Avery assured her as the ladies helped her get dressed and led her to the car.

"Where are you going to take her?" asked Meesha.

"Since she doesn't want to go to Adverse General I'm going to take her to Miami Grace."

"Okay, I'll meet you there," Peyton said. "Meesha do you want to ride with me?"

"Why don't you let me drive. You just had that procedure yesterday."

"I'm good. I only had to rest for a day."

"Yea, but this is a stressful situation, and I don't want you taking any unnecessary chances. Come on," Meesha insisted and Peyton followed her to her car.

Ω

Hours later, the doctor came in to talk to Eva. Peyton, Avery, and Meesha surrounded her.

"Mrs. Stenberg, we've run tests. First, I want to address your physical condition. You don't have any broken bones but you do have severe bruising of the ribs. You're lucky too that your eye socket wasn't detached. Whoever did this to you, well let's just say I hope you've reported this assault to the police.

Eva said nothing, but instead looked around at each of her friends and back to the doctor.

The doctor followed her eyes and looked at the ladies too as if seeking answers to who had caused her injuries.

"I strongly urge you to report this. You could be dead right now."

Eva cried, something she'd basically been doing since before they left to take her to the hospital. She couldn't seem to stop.

"I'm going to give you something for your pain. I hate to tell you this, but we were unable to save your baby. I'm so sorry."

Eva was stunned. For the first time she looked at the doctor eye to eye. "What did you say? Baby? I'm not pregnant."

Avery, Meesha, and Peyton eyed each other.

"Hold up," she was pregnant?" said Peyton, staring boldly at the doctor and then reverting her eyes toward Eva.

"You didn't know?" he asked Eva.

"But...I...I can't be. Uh, I mean I couldn't have been pregnant. My husband is sterile. He had a vasectomy."

"You were pregnant, Mrs. Stenberg. But unfortunately you lost the child. And it's most likely due to the assault you sustained. I see bruises on your belly, shoe prints to be exact." The doctor shook his head and patted Eva's hand gently. "We need to perform a minor surgical procedure called a D and C. It will remove any remaining tissue. I'd like to admit you and keep you overnight just for continued observation. I want to make sure no complications arise from the amount of injuries you've sustained or from the procedure."

Eva nodded.

"The nurse will be back in shortly to get you prepared for surgery and to admit you into the hospital. Any questions?"

"Are...are you sure I was pregnant?"

"One hundred percent."

When the doctor exited the room, the ladies gathered close to Eva's bed.

"Did you sleep with someone else?" Peyton asked as only Peyton would do.

"No, no. I would never make that mistake again."

"Then, how? I mean, what?" Avery said, totally confused and baffled by the revelation.

"I don't understand," said Meesha. "Harper had a vasectomy."

"Duh, obviously the man lied. Unless he's some kind of miracle making baby maker. I knew it. That scumbag has been lying the whole time about being sterile," surmised Peyton.

Eva cried into her hands. The housewives did their best to console her.

The door opened and two nurses appeared.

"Mrs. Stenberg?"

Eva nodded.

"Let me check your arm for your name," one of them said.

The housewives stepped back, allowing the nurse access to Eva. After she was done, she asked Eva a few questions, and the other one checked her IV.

"Okay, we're going to take you for the D and C. After the procedure is done you'll be taken to your room," one of them explained. "You all can get her room number from the desk in the waiting room. You'll be able to wait on her in her room or in the waiting room area."

"Thank you," Meesha said.

Both nurses smiled. "You ready?" one of them said.

"Yes, I'm ready," Eva said softly, wiping away tears.

27

"Find your tribe. Love them hard."
Everyday Blog

Eva put up a fuss but the housewives were finally able to convince her that going to Meesha's would be best. Eva was discharged the following afternoon and for the past three days she'd been staying there.

She hadn't heard from Harper since he left, which was somewhat unusual and that made her a little on edge. Sometimes when she didn't hear from him when he was out of town, he called himself surprising her and coming home unannounced. She prayed this wouldn't be the case.

Still recovering from her injuries and the fact the doctor told her she had a miscarriage, Eva was a nervous wreck. Harper had lied to her from the very beginning about having a vasectomy. Who had she married? He was not at all like the man she believed he was. This Harper was cunning, abusive, cruel and downright mean. Yet, he had a way of trying to cover his sins by showering her with expensive gifts and tokens. Well, she was sick and tired of it. To think that he had been the cause for her miscarriage sent her spiraling into a deep dark place. Thoughts of suicide raced through her mind. Why was her life worth living? She didn't see any hope.

"Things are going to work out, Eva," Meesha told her as they sat in the family room. It was raining outside, the boys were in their playroom, and Meesha held Makena Grace in her arms.

"I wish I could believe that, Meesha. This is not what I expected my life to be like in America and being married to Harper. I had foolish pictures in my mind of being married happily ever after, but look at me. I'm beaten down physically, mentally, and spiritually. How could I ever believe God loves me, Meesha? What have I done that was so bad for him to hate me?"

Makena snuggled up against her mother. "Now you listen to me, Eva. God does not hate you. God loves you. Yes, things may be bad for you right now, but you watch what I tell you, God is going to turn your situation around. He's going to make everything right. I know you don't see it right now, and you may not believe what I'm saying, but it's the truth. Harper has to pay. He will pay. He's running up in church Sunday after Sunday, jumping up shouting and dancing and then he gets home and he abuses and lies to his wife. It's not right and he's going to have to pay."

"Why did God let me lose my baby?" Eva cried.

"I don't pretend to have all the answers as to why God allows things to happen the way they do. All I know is he's going to give you beauty for your ashes."

Eva's cell phone rang. She looked at it and answered it.

"Hey, Eva."

"Hi, Peyton. How are you feeling?"

"Hopeless."

"Eva, don't do this. Don't allow Harper to bring you down like this."

"I can't help it. I lost a baby, a baby I didn't even know I was carrying."

"I know. I know, but please, Eva. You have to pull yourself out of this slump."

"I don't know how, Peyton. I need to go back to Bolivia. Harper is going to be back in a few days and I don't know what he's going to do when he comes home and finds me gone."

"That's what I was calling about. Have you talked to Avery?"

"No, not today. Why?"

"I'll let her tell you. I just wanted to check on you. Do you need anything?"

"No, but thanks, Peyton."

"No problem. I'll check on you later tonight or tomorrow. Okay?"

"Okay." Eva ended the call. "That was Peyton."

"Yea, I heard."

The phone rang again and this time it was Avery.

"Hey."

"Hey, Eva. How are you feeling?"

"Still sore and hurting."

"I know you're going to probably get upset when I tell you this, but at this point I had to do something."

"What did you do?" Eva looked over at Meesha.

Meesha shrugged, an indication she had no idea what Avery was saying.

"I talked to Ryker. I told him everything. He was livid. He couldn't believe Harper was the monster he is."

"Why would you do that? Why would you tell Ryker about Harper when I asked you, begged you, not to, Avery?"

"Because you need help. He says you should file an order of protection against Harper. That'll bar him from coming anywhere near you and keep him from the house too. You can live in some peace until you decide what you want to do. He said he would go with you and file the necessary paperwork."

"I don't know about an order of protection."

Meesha's ears perked. She looked at Eva, nodded, and mouthed, "Do it."

Eva shrugged, tilted her head, and raised up a hand in doubt.

"Look, I want you to talk to Ryker. He can tell you what's involved. Will you just talk to him?"

"I guess. Sure."

"Okay, I'll pick you up tomorrow and we'll go to his office. Okay?"

"Okay."

"Now get some rest. We'll talk later."

"Sure. Bye," Eva said.

"She wants you to file an order of protection from what I heard."

"Yea, she does."

"And you don't want to do that after the man has beaten you and caused you to lose your child? Come on now, Eva. You can't allow your fear of Harper to paralyze you, to allow him to wreak havoc in your life at his will. Next time you may not be so lucky; he'll kill you."

Eva listened. Maybe her friends were right. Maybe this protection order could protect her."

"Avery is going to pick me up tomorrow and take me to Ryker's office. I'll see what he has to say and find out what his order can do."

"Good for you," Meesha said, exhaled and put Makena down on the floor. The little girl took off waddling across the floor. She had started to walk just days ago. Meesha used her phone to take a video of her precious baby girl.

"She's so beautiful," Eva said and managed a light laugh.

"Yep, she's my little mini me."

Makena Grace toddled around for a few feet then plopped down on her bottom and started crawling. She went straight to Eva and began pulling up on Eva's leg.

Eva smiled, picked up the little girl, and held her in her arms. It hurt but she tried her hardest to dismiss the pain.

"Hey, *chica bonita.* You are such a pretty girl."

Makena moved against Eva, pressing her chubby fingers into Eva's chest and kicking against her belly. Eva winced.

"She's hurting you. Let me get her." Meesha leaned over and Eva passed Makena into her arms.

"Why don't you go upstairs and get some rest."

"Maybe I will. I am tired."

211

Eva's phone rang again. This time she frowned and sighed.

Meesha knew it had to be Harper on the phone because Eva's face became flushed.

Eva barely gave him time to speak before she lit into him with an anger that was totally unlike her. She screamed and cried as she told him about the miscarriage.

"You lied! You've been lying to me all this time. Why? Why would you do this?"

"You're the liar. You couldn't have been pregnant by me. I told you I had a vasectomy," he yelled back.

"I haven't slept with anyone but you. I hate you. You caused me to lose our child. I'll never forgive you, Harper Stenberg. Not ever!" She ended the call but right away her phone started ringing again.

"Don't you ever hang up on me. Do you hear me?"

"I hate you. I want a divorce." She ended the call again and then turned to Meesha. "I need that protection order or else he's going to kill me."

28

"Hateful to me as the gates of Hades is that man who hides one thing in his heart and speaks another." Homer

Carlton took his Sunday message from 1 Corinthians 13, better known as the *love chapter*. As he hooped and hollered and paced across the pulpit, an aching emptiness filled his heart when he saw the pew where Meesha usually sat was empty. This was the second Sunday his wife and kids were missing from church and they hadn't been to midweek service either.

He had called her nonstop and texted her too, but she refused to answer. He also noticed her friends and their spouses weren't at church either. He had been praying and asking God for help. So far God seemed silent. Could he blame him?

Evelyn told him about Meesha's pop up visit to her and Martin's house. Boy was he glad Evelyn was with him that night and not at home. That would have been a huge fiasco had she been there. Now Meesha had threatened to expose him and Evelyn if he tried to come back home. For now he had to play the game her way until he figured out what he needed to do.

How could he have let his guard down and been caught slipping? He always thought he was safe doing his thing in Miami. Boy, had that been proven wrong. Whenever he messed off on Meesha he was usually far more careful. This time he had been caught and with all people, Evelyn, his brother's wife.

During the week after Meesha threw him out, he did go see the boys at the Academy and that gave him some solace, but Meesha was absent from the Academy as well, and he missed his sweet little baby girl. He explained to his sons that their mother and him were going through a rough patch but he would be back home real soon.

His oldest son, CJ, was at that age where he understood divorce. He had friends whose parents were divorced. He missed his dad being in the house and he hoped he was telling them the truth about coming back soon.

When Carlton went to Meesha's office, he didn't ask anyone about her whereabouts. That would most likely raise suspicion if the pastor didn't know his own wife wasn't at work.

He was furious that Meesha banned him from his own home, but one thing about Meesha, once she set her mind to something she was going to carry it out. He couldn't take any chances with her spilling the beans to his brother.

After Sunday service ended, a number of members asked about his family, wondering if First Lady Meesha and the kids were okay. Carlton reassured them his family was fine. If only that was true.

"Hey, bruh, where's the fam?" his brother Kingston asked after the church was cleared and most of the stragglers had left.

"Uh, Makena wasn't feeling too well. She has a cold and the boys started complaining too, so Meesha wanted to stay at home with them to make sure they were good. You know how that goes, man."

"They didn't miss school last week so they must not be too sick," Kingston joked.

Martin appeared and Carlton felt uneasy but the three brothers laughed and talked about the upcoming game and mixed that with sports talk about Perfecting Your Faith's championship football team. It helped take Carlton's mind off his dilemma, but he knew it wouldn't be long before his double life could be exposed. He would be the loser in that game if that were to happen.

He had to put his A game on to get Meesha to listen to him and to keep her from going to

Martin. In the meantime, he had been staying at the Setai Hotel until he could worm his way back home.

Ω

Meesha hadn't been bothered by Carlton, and she knew why. She warned him if he tried to come back to the house she was going to tell Martin everything about him and Evelyn and show him the pictures. She had an appointment with the attorney Ryker set her up with and she was ready to file for divorce. There was nothing Carlton could do to make her change her mind. All she wanted was everything she could get and then some from his sorry, cheating behind.

The lawyer she was seeing was known as The Beast. She was supposed to be just that good. *You messed with the wrong one this time, Carlton.*

The one thing bothering Meesha since she caught her husband and Evelyn were the nightmares. They had returned and most nights it was hard, and sometimes impossible, to get any sleep. Thoughts of Terrell and of all people, Breyonna, tormented her almost every night for the past week, and Meesha didn't know why. Was God trying to tell her something? She had her own secret sins, that was evident with the returning dreams of Terrell, but what about Breyonna? Why would she be dreaming about her? Could there be more to the Breyonna situation than she knew? Was there more to Carlton's story about her? There was so much she began to realize she didn't know about her husband. Maybe his secrets would be revealed, but if that meant exposing hers, it might be best she let some sleeping dogs lie.

29

"Sometimes the only thing you can do for people is to be there." Terry Pratchett

Ryker had submitted the petition for an order of protection. The judge issued a temporary injunction against Harper.

Eva was on pins and needles because Harper had returned the day before and was served order of protection papers within an hour or so after he came back. Thanks went to Marissa who called and told Eva the moment he returned. She was still staying at Meesha's but that would be coming to an end if she received a permanent order of protection, which Ryker assured her she would.

She didn't know if Harper would show up to the hearing, but again Ryker explained it didn't matter if Harper appeared in court or not. It only mattered that he was served with the papers and information about the hearing.

Marissa told her when Harper received the papers he went into a rage, destroying several things around the house, including removing most of Eva's clothing from the house. She told Eva she didn't know what he did with them. Hearing this terrified Eva even more until she had second thoughts about the decision she'd made to issue the order.

Today was the moment of truth—the hearing. Eva would have to testify. Facing this was what unnerved her the most. Seeing Harper sitting in front of her while she had to tell the judge the unspeakable abuse she'd suffered at his hands was going to be tough, if not downright impossible. Could she do it? Could she expose the sick, vile side of what the public saw as an amazing, gifted surgeon, author, and TV host?

Her friends told her she had the strength to do it, and Ryker assured her if she wanted the order she would have to speak up.

"You can do this," Avery reassured Eva.

"Yes, it's time for you to take your life back," Meesha encouraged as they prepared to go to court.

Maybe Harper wouldn't show up. That would be the perfect scenario because the judge could grant a default judgment. But knowing Harper the way she thought she knew him, he would be there and intimidate her with his presence.

Ω

Entering the courtroom, Meesha, Peyton, and Avery surrounded her like she was a celebrity star. Thank God, the news hadn't reached the media or else her private business would be scattered across social media and the news. Harper was a big deal in Adverse City and the country, and this would be a huge blow to his career. Not that she cared about his career one way or the other after the way he had treated her

Eva still couldn't get over the realization Harper wasn't sterile. Every day she cried over the loss of her child, a child she blamed him for killing. She could never forgive him for that.

When she entered the courtroom and she didn't see Harper she released a pinned up sigh. *Thank you, God he isn't here.* Her joy didn't last long, because minutes before her case was to be heard, in walked Harper flanked by his own little entourage. That's the only way she could explain it. It made her uneasy because he seemed to be flaunting his power and control over her life.

When Ryker called her to come to the witness stand her nerves and intense anxiety almost got the best of her. As she approached the stand her legs felt like pudding, her palms became sweaty, and her face clouded with uneasiness.

When Ryker addressed the issues of abuse she suffered at the hands of Harper, she swallowed hard trying to avoid Harper's penetrating stare.

Thinking about how he was the cause of her losing her baby was what gave her the strength and resolve she needed to tell the judge every single detail about Harper's abuse. The more she talked the more she began feeling a sense of relief. Tears poured from her eyes as she told about how he'd kicked and stomped her, causing her to lose her baby. She told the judge about his lies about having a vasectomy, about the nights, days, and mornings he would beat her sometimes to unconsciousness. How he forced her to engage in sex after his beatings. She testified to all of this and at the end she returned Harper's murderous stare with one of her own. She had found her strength. She had spoken out against the man she once loved but who was now her number one nemesis.

Listening to Eva describe what she'd gone through caused the housewives to cringe. They had no idea the amount of abuse their friend had suffered at Harper's hands. It became too much for Meesha and midway through the hearing she bolted out of the courtroom. She didn't return until toward the end, just in time to hear the judge's decision.

After chastising Harper for the despicable acts he'd subjected his wife to and how he had brought shame to the medical profession, the judge granted Eva a two-year order of protection. He further explained to Harper he could no longer reside at the home he and Eva once called home.

After thanking Ryker for his representation, Eva and the housewives exited the courtroom, without Eva so much as giving Harper a glance. She had won, at least this first round. She wouldn't allow herself to think about what was ahead, but she knew divorce was imminent.

Ryker had referred her to the same divorce attorney he referred to Meesha, and Eva was going to make an appointment in the next few weeks.

For now, she was happy she would be able to return to the only place she knew as home. Like Meesha, she was going to change the locks, security codes, and gate access as a double measure of security.

Ω

The ladies celebrated Eva's victory by going to Red's.

"We're proud of you," Avery said first as the ladies waited at Red's for their meal orders.

Eva smiled big.

"Yes, you found your voice," said Peyton. "I couldn't believe it. I said to myself, finally the little birdie sings." Peyton laughed and then grew serious. "Sitting in that courtroom and hearing what all you went through, I want to say I'm so sorry, Eva. I only wish you had told us sooner, when Harper first laid hands on you."

"I know, and I wish I had told you all sooner, but I was ashamed and scared."

Avery reached next to her where Eva sat and patted her hand for reassurance. "I'm just thankful you came out of this alive."

"But I lost my baby," Eva said, almost beginning to cry but she held her tears at bay.

"I know you did and that was horrible that he made you lose it, but God knows what he's doing. Rest assured of that," Meesha told her.

"And I'm worried about my family in Bolivia. I know Harper is cutting them off."

"Girl, please. That should be your least worry. We already told you we got you. I talked to Derek, and he's setting up an account specifically for us so we can deposit money into it. Your parents won't have to worry about a thing."

"Yea, we got you. We're going to put money in it every month," added Meesha.

"And the restaurant is going to bring in even more money, so forget about Harper," Peyton reassured her.

"Oh, my God," Eva cried, unable to hold back her tears any longer. "I love you all so much. Thank you for being my friends."

"It never hurts to have rich friends, really rich friends," joked Peyton and burst out laughing.

The other housewives, including Eva joined her.

"Just know that better is coming, Eva. And you know what?" said Meesha.

"What?" replied Eva.

"You've given me my voice, too. I've made up my mind. I'm not going to keep silent. It's time I clue Martin in on what his brother and wife have been doing behind his back." Meesha picked up her club soda and took a swallow.

"That's what I'm talking about, girl," Peyton said. "Let's toast."

The ladies raised their glasses and clicked them together. "To good times ahead."

30

"Sometimes doors open and others close and you have to figure out which one you're going to take." Gisele Bundchen

Peyton and Derek sat in the doctor's office waiting to be called back. This was the day of her pregnancy test and she couldn't be more excited and nervous.

Derek squeezed her hand trying to reassure his wife, hoping he was hiding his own heightened anxiety.

Liam came along too, but like always his head was in his phone and his earbuds in his ears.

"Mrs. Hudson," the nurse called.

Peyton and Derek got up. Derek touched Liam on his shoulder.

Removing one earbud, Liam said, "Is it time?"

"Yes, son. We're about to find out if you're going to have a little brother or sister to get on your nerves." Derek chuckled and Liam stood and followed.

"You might want your son to wait in the waiting room until the test is completed," the nurse said.

"Cool," Liam said and quickly turned back around and reclaimed his seat.

Inside the room, Derek kissed his wife.

Dr. Thomas entered shortly after they were placed inside the room. "You ready to find out if you're pregnant?" Dr. Thomas asked, smiling.

"Yes, we are," Peyton said, looking at Derek, who kissed her again.

Dr. Thomas drew blood and afterwards instructed Peyton to go to the bathroom so she could collect a urine sample. When she returned from the bathroom, she and Derek held hands, anticipating the door opening and Dr. Thomas walking in to give them the results.

"Do you want me to get Liam?" Derek asked.

"I don't know. What do you think? I mean suppose I'm not pregnant? I don't want him to see my disappointment."

"Hey, we're not going to think like that. We're keeping the faith. If it turns out you're not, Liam is just as important to this as you and I are."

"You're right. Okay, you can bring him back."

"If Dr. Thomas comes in here don't let her give you the results until we're back."

"I won't," Peyton reassured her husband.

When he left out of the room, Peyton relaxed on the exam table, relishing thoughts of how happy she was at this moment. If she wasn't pregnant, she told herself there was always another chance for her because she still had frozen embryos. If she was pregnant then she and Derek could use the frozen embryos at a later time in case they wanted to get pregnant again. All in all though she prayed this first time was the charm and that Dr. Thomas would walk in the room and tell her she was carrying Derek's child.

Derek and Liam returned and not a moment too soon because right after they entered the room Dr. Thomas appeared.

"What's the verdict, Doc?" Derek asked, massaging his own hands before reaching out and grabbing hold of Peyton's.

Peyton sucked in a deep breath and then slowly released it while Liam stood on the opposite side of his mom looking unbothered and cool as a cucumber.

Anticipation hung over the room like a cloud. Peyton closed her eyes momentarily then opened them. She squeezed Derek's hand as hard as she could.

"Well, Mrs. Hudson...Mr. Hudson," Dr. Thomas looked at Derek and then at Liam, "you are pregnant."

"Oh, my God. Oh my God!" Peyton screamed and kept screaming as she hugged Derek. She jumped down off the table and Liam ran around to his mother and father. The three of them embraced and jumped up and down in total joy.

"It's a miracle. Thank you, God," Derek cried. "Thank you."

"Congratulations, Mom and Dad," Liam said.

"Thank you, son." Derek kissed his son hard on the cheek.

Peyton then kissed him too. "I'm so glad you were here to witness this. I love you so much, Liam."

"Love you too, Mom."

"What's next, Dr. Thomas?" asked Derek.

"Well, you're not done with us yet, Mrs. Hudson. We still have to keep a close eye on you. We're going to have to do blood work every three days to make sure your pregnancy hormone is rising at the level it should and that your progesterone levels are adequate to sustain a pregnancy. After about five and half weeks into your pregnancy, we'll administer an ultrasound to make sure everything is progressing normally. We'll also check for a multiple pregnancy."

"Multiple pregnancy? Oh my, gosh. I didn't think about that," said Peyton, placing a hand over her mouth in surprise while Derek smiled and Liam's eyes bucked.

"Yes, multiple pregnancy," Dr. Thomas said. You'll come here for weekly, ultrasounds after that so we can evaluate the progress of your pregnancy. You'll even be able to see the embryo or embryos," she paused and smiled, "growing and hear the heartbeat. After eight to ten weeks, that's when I'll discharge you from my care and you will start being seen by an OB GYN. I have an excellent one I can refer you to. That is, unless you already have one in mind."

Both Peyton and Derek shook their heads. "No, we don't. Whoever you recommend that's who we'll go with."

"Good. Well, if you don't have any questions, I'll see you in three days. You can schedule your appointments up front before you leave."

"Thank you, Dr. Thomas."

Derek reached out and shook the doctor's hand.

"Congratulations again," Dr. Thomas said and exited the room.

Peyton allowed her tears to flow and she and Derek embraced again.

"I'm hungry. Can we stop somewhere on the way home and get something to eat?" Liam asked.

They pulled apart and both of them looked at Liam and smiled. "You can have whatever you want, big brother," Derek said, swatting his son on the back.

"Yep, sure can. Whatever you like, wherever you like," Peyton said.

31

"The best revenge is just moving on and getting over it. Don't give someone the satisfaction of watching you suffer." Unknown

Avery was in a good place. For the first time in a very long time, she could honestly say she was happy and content. She and Ryker were doing better than ever. Everything was all good.

Her phone rang while she was playing with RJ. It was Eva.

"Hey, girl."

"Hey, what's going on?"

"Not much. I wanted to know if you want to do a little shopping. I told you Harper threw out just about every stitch of clothing, make-up, jewelry, everything I had. I need to go re-up and I want to find something special for the restaurant opening."

"Okay, sounds good. You inviting Meesha and Peyton?"

Eva's text pinged. "Yes, I was going to call them after I talked to you. Peyton just texted me. I want to see what news she's got. I hope it's good."

"Me too. Oh, hold up. She just texted me, too."

Both of the ladies started screaming into the phone almost at the same time when they read Peyton's text: "You wanches finna be godmommas!"

"Ahhh, I'm so happy for her and Derek," gushed Eva.

"Me too. This definitely calls for some retail therapy and some good food."

"You right about that. Let me group text Peyton and Meesha. I'll add you too and see if they want to get together."

"Okay. If they don't I'll still go with you."

"Okay. See you soon."

Eva ended the call and proceeded to group text the ladies. She was feeling accomplished. The renovations on the restaurant were nearing an end. They had been posting information on social media, running cable, TV and radio advertisements about the grand opening, and had a street team distributing flyers. She felt better than she had in a long time. She had met with the divorce attorney and surprisingly she hadn't received a text or a single phone call from Harper. At first she was nervous and scared returning to the house, but now a week later she was more at ease, happy she'd faced her enemy right in the face and won.

The divorce attorney contacted Harper who referred him to his own attorney. After conferring with him, Harper was ordered to pay Eva spousal support on a temporary basis during the divorce proceedings. On top of that he was not to discontinue any of the credit cards he had given her and he had to continue the mortgage payments, car note, and all other expenses on the home, which included Marissa's salary. Eva didn't know her own strength, hadn't recognized her power until the day she found the courage to step up on that stand. From that day on she began to feel like she had a future, a real future apart from Harper.

Her text message pinged. Peyton and Meesha said they would love to meet up and do some damage in the stores.

"Can't wait to tell y'all about my night," Meesha texted.

Ω

It was one of the best days ever for Peyton and Eva. Being with their friends, celebrating with laughter, shopping, fun and food was all that and more. They discussed the final plans for the soft opening of Eva and Friends Bolivian Cuisine. The public grand opening would follow the day after. The private opening was going to be a stellar affair, complete with red carpet and the who's who of Adverse City and Miami. The ladies were on cloud nine about it.

"Peyton, girl I'm so happy for you and Derek," Meesha congratulated.

"I am too," Avery and then Eva said.

"And you say you might have multiples?" asked Eva.

"Yep, it's a chance," Peyton said, laughing.

"Girl, that would be amazing. After all this time you and Derek are going to have a kid—" said Meesha.

"Or kids," interrupted Avery.

"Of your own," finished Meesha.

"That's wild," said Eva.

"Yea, I know," Peyton said. "But enough about me. I want to hear what you have to tell us. Did you do it?" Peyton asked Meesha.

"I think you ladies would be proud of me. I blew that thing out the water!" Meesha exclaimed.

"I paid a visit *again*, unannounced, to my brother-in-law and his cheating skank of a wife."

The housewives' eyes lit up.

"No you didn't," said Avery, glad Carlton Porter was going to get what was due him.

"Oh, yes I did. You could have bought that broad for a penny when she answered the door and saw me standing on the other side."

"What happened next?" asked Eva.

"She couldn't help but invite me in because Martin walked up. I walked up in that house like I owned it. The first thing I asked them was if the kids were home. They were, but Martin said they were upstairs getting ready for bed.

Meesha continued telling the ladies what transpired.

Perfect, Meesha said in her mind and followed Martin and Evelyn to the family room where Martin offered her a seat.

"What's going on, Meesha?" Martin asked.

"I need to talk to you about something. Something very important and private. I don't want the kids to hear."

"Meesha, if it's that critical why not wait until the kids aren't home or you and I can meet up somewhere, have lunch, tomorrow," Evelyn suggested, struggling to keep herself deceptively controlled while Meesha laughed inside.

"No, this can't wait. As a matter of fact, Martin, why don't you call your brother? I'm sure he'll want to be here for this."

"What's going on, Meesha? I know you and Carlton are having problems, but I was hoping it was temporary" Martin said.

"Oh, indeed we are, Martin. We're having serious problems." She cut her eyes toward Evelyn.

A boom of thunder rolled and Evelyn jumped, startled. For a minute Meesha and Evelyn's eyes met and her mouth took on an unpleasant twist.

Meesha laughed a haughty laugh as she leaned back in the chair, relatively calm and relaxed.

"Um, sounds like that thunderstorm they've been predicting is settling in," Martin said.

"Yes, it sure is, but it'll be okay. I'm going to say what I have to say and get on out of here. Are you going to call Carlton?"

"Sure. If you and Carlton need to talk to us about your marriage, Evelyn and I are here for you. Right, babe?" He reached out and placed his hand over Evelyn's.

"Yes, but I just think whatever's going on between you and Carlton is really none of our business," Evelyn said. "Martin and I don't like interfering with other people's personal

problems. That is unless someone comes to us for prayer."

"But, babe, Meesha and Carlton are family. If they need us we should be here for them."

"Thank you, Martin. You've such a good brother-in-law."

"Now let me call that knucklehead brother of mine. Let me go get my phone. You two talk. I'll be right back." Martin stood up and walked out.

"What is this about, Meesha?" Evelyn asked. Her expression a mask of stone.

"You know darn well what this is about. Don't play me, Evelyn. I'm here to tell your husband everything."

Evelyn's tone softened. "Please, don't do this, Meesha. You'll ruin my marriage, break up my family."

"Don't beg now. You didn't think of that when you were banging my husband. Did you ever think what it would do to me to find out about you and Carlton? Here, look at this, Evelyn." She opened her phone gallery and passed her phone to Evelyn.

Evelyn looked at the images of her and Carlton. One showed Carlton's hand on her butt. Another one showed them kissing.

"Please, Meesha. It was nothing. Just a short fling, a one-time thing. Martin and I were having some problems and Carlton, well things just *went from one thing to the other. I would never intentionally hurt you. You're a good woman, Meesha."*

"I don't need you to tell me what kind of woman I am, Evelyn. And how dare you sit here and lie to my face when you know you've been sleeping with my low down, cheating, scheming husband for God knows how long."

Out the corner of her eye Meesha saw Martin appear but she kept talking. He stopped in the doorway, obviously hearing what she said, but she pretended like she didn't see him.

Evelyn's back was turned so she had no idea her husband was standing in the doorway behind her.

"You want to beg me not to tell Martin but what about me, Evelyn? What about my family, my marriage, my kids? How could you betray me like this, better yet, how could you cheat on a man as good as Martin? And do it with his own brother?"

Evelyn began crying. "I'm sorry, believe me I am, Meesha."

"Yea, you're sorry all right."

Martin ran into the room and Meesha feigned surprise. "Martin, I...I'm sorry you."

"Don't be sorry, Meesha. Is what she said true, Evelyn? Have you been sleeping with my brother?" His face was marked with loathing as

the storm picked up its pace and the rain pounded against the house and windows. The wind released a mighty roar, but it was nothing compared to what was going on inside the Porter household.

"Martin, please. It's not what you think."

"Not what I think? You've been sleeping with my brother?" His expression was tight with strain and his eyes turned icy cold.

Evelyn jumped up from the sofa and ran up to her husband, trying to take hold of his hand but he pulled away.

Martin chuckled nastily. "How could you, Evelyn?"

"Martin, please." Evelyn felt suddenly weak and vulnerable in the face of his anger.

Meesha watched Martin's heart breaking into a million pieces. She felt his pain because it happened to her. Carlton had torn her heart in two and she didn't think it would ever come together again.

The doorbell rung and Martin rushed to the door. Meesha and Evelyn heard the yelling as soon as he opened it.

Next there was a loud ruckus in the foyer. Meesha jumped up from her chair and Evelyn took off to the foyer.

Martin was pounding Carlton over and over. Carlton fought back but the blows his brother landed had taken him off guard and he landed on the floor.

The kids ran downstairs but right away Evelyn ordered them to go back to their rooms and not come back downstairs.

"Stop. Stop it," Evelyn screamed, stepping in and trying to tear the men apart.

Meesha watched as Martin finally released Carlton and he got up from the floor, his nose bloody. He wiped the blood with the back of his hand.

"I don't know what Meesha told you, but bruh, it was nothing, absolutely nothing between Evelyn and me." Looking over his shoulder, his shirt torn and his eyes glooming, Evelyn answered.

"I told you, Martin. It was nothing, baby."

"And you both stand here lying to my face. How could you, bro? You dirty bas--. You dirty dog," he said instead of cussing

"How long?" He glowered at Carlton.

Carlton said nothing but quickly glanced at Evelyn. Then he turned to Meesha. "Is this what you wanted? To destroy my brother? To cause him pain like this?"

"Don't you try to blame this on me, Carlton. You did this. You and her," Meesha said, looking at Evelyn. "I'll leave the three of you to settle this, but before I go, just in case they try to weasel out of this like they're trying to do now, take a look at these, Martin." She passed the phone toward Martin but before he could get it, Carlton ran up and smacked the phone out of Meesha's hand.

Meesha laughed, and when Carlton tried to pick it up, Martin pushed him aside and got the phone. He looked at picture after picture with disgust and his broad carved face twisted in anger.

"My God," he said with a voice that had suddenly turned quiet, but held an undertone of cold contempt.

When he was done looking at the pictures he passed the phone back to Meesha.

Meesha saw his eyes had darkened like the very thunderclouds outside. Without saying anything else, she walked to the door that was still open. "Martin, remember this, when a man steals your wife, there is no better revenge than to let him keep her." With that being said, she fiercely walked outside into the raging storm. Her mission complete.

Peyton was the first to speak up after Meesha finished telling her story. "Girl, I can't believe it. I didn't know you had it in you. You and Eva have really surprised me lately."

"Have you heard from him, Evelyn, or Martin?"

"Nope. What is there for them to say? I mean, I feel sorry for my brother-in-law, but it wasn't right for me to suffer in silence and let what they did slide.

"No, you did right," said Avery. "Carlton deserved it."

Eva shot Avery a quick glance, slightly shaking her head.

Peyton noticed the exchange between the two ladies but said nothing. Had something gone down that Avery or Eva weren't telling her or Meesha? Had Eva slept with Carlton? Avery? Something had happened but Peyton quickly dismissed those thoughts and returned back to the conversation at hand.

"Yes, cheating on you with his brother's wife was wrong. So wrong," Eva said.

"Yep, on all levels," added Peyton.

"You know what? I can't believe I haven't sunk into a depression after learning this. But I'm okay. I've been praying about it. The divorce is in process and I'm good. I'm confident God's going to provide for me and my kids. He says all things work together for good for those who love the Lord and are called according to His purpose. He's going to take care of me. I take that back, He already *is* taking care of me and mine. As for Reverend

Carlton Porter, he is going to have his day in court. Bet that."

"Cheers to that," said Avery and the other housewives agreed.

32

"Do one thing every day that scares you."
Anonymous

The soft opening went off without a hitch. Media was everywhere and celebrities and Adverse City socialites showed up in full force. People raved about Eva's delicious cuisine. Happiness filled her as she interacted with the guests.

Her heart jolted and her pulse pounded when she saw Quentin, his brother and his brother's wife, and Emma Winters on the red carpet.

When they left the red carpet, they stopped and intermingled with other guests until a hostess approached them and showed them to their reserved seats.

The renovators had done an excellent job of turning the Mexican restaurant into an elegant, upper class, dining establishment.

Eva continued walking around, checking on guests and enjoying the whole scene.

Avery, Meesha, and Peyton were enjoying themselves as well. Ryker and Derek were proud of their wives and the idea of opening a restaurant to support Eva.

Eva made it over to Emma Winters' table. "Good evening, Mrs. Winters. I'm so glad you and your family could be here." Her grandson and his wife spoke and then Quentin.

"Hello, Eva. This is nice. I'm impressed," Quentin said and smiled a dashing smile.

"Nice, phooey," said Mrs. Winters. "Darling, this restaurant is beautiful and these appetizers are exquisite. You and your friends have done an outstanding job. This is going to be the go to place for the best cuisine in Miami. I'm going to see to that. Are you the one responsible for this menu?" Emma asked.

"Yes, ma'am."

"Hello, Mrs. Winters," Derek said, walking up to the table, leaning down and kissing Emma Winters on the cheek.

"Darling, Derek. It is so good to see you," she blushed and smiled. Grabbing hold of his hand, she kissed it.

"I hope you're enjoying yourself. Is everything to your liking?"

"Yes," she said, clapping her hands together. "I was just telling Eva I'm going to make sure this is the go to place. The food is heavenly. The atmosphere, well, everything is just magical."

"I'm glad you like it. I wanted to come over and speak. Peyton should be over shortly. If

245

you need anything, please stop one of the hostesses and let them know." He kissed her cheek again before excusing himself to continue mingling with the other guests.

Returning her focus to Eva, Emma Winters continued to praise her. "Quentin told me about your plans to open a restaurant. You're off to a good start, dear. I see bigger and better things in your future if you keep this up."

"Ohhh, thank you, Mrs. Winters." Eva noticed Quentin watching her intently and a ripple of excitement rushed through her. "Thank you so much. That means a lot coming from you."

"I'm just stating the truth. And please, call me Emma, darling."

"Yes—Emma."

"You look beautiful this evening, Mrs. Stenberg," Quentin admired.

Trying not to stumble over her words, she spoke carefully. "Th...thank you, Mr. Winters."

"Where is Harper? I haven't seen him around?" Emma Winters interrupted.

"Uh, I'm afraid he won't be able to make it tonight."

"Hogwash. You mean to tell me that man is not here on his wife's opening night? I've got a serious bone to pick with him," Emma Winters said, huffing in obvious disgust.

Eva smiled but said nothing in response. This was not the time or place to go into the reason for Harper's absence. Sooner or later Emma Winters would find out about her and Harper's impending divorce but Eva was not going to be the one to tell her.

"Well, if you'll excuse me, I need to make sure everything is going as it should in the kitchen."

Quentin got up from the table and followed her. "Why haven't you been returning my calls and texts? Did I do something?"

Eva stopped, looked around, and caught the eye of Avery who winked, nodded, and smiled as if giving her approval.

"Uh, no. It's nothing like that. It's just that, well things have been so hectic. It's taken every waking moment to get to this point. You should know that, Quentin. This is your field of expertise."

"I do know that. But after you told me you couldn't work at the shelter anymore, I talked to you one time after that and poof, it's like you totally disappeared. I thought we were friends, Eva."

"We are. I guess."

"You guess? What's going on? You know you can talk to me. I know Harper had a lot to do with you quitting the shelter. Did he tell you to stay away from me too? And what's the real reason he isn't here?"

"Quentin, you're asking too many questions. Questions I can't answer. This isn't the place or time."

"I've been in New York and France for the past two months taking care of my own restaurants, but I'm back now, Eva. And I've missed you like crazy."

Her heart thudded and a quiver surged through her veins. Being close to him was like a drug, lulling her into euphoria. She had to get away.

"I told you, I can't do this now, Quentin. Now if you'll excuse me, I need to check on the kitchen staff." Swiftly, she turned and walked off, leaving Quentin watching her until she was out of his sight.

He didn't know what was going on with Eva, but he was not going to leave things as they were. He cared about her, liked her, and he wanted to be part of her life anyway he could.

Turning to walk back to his table, Avery approached him and officially introduced herself and welcomed him to the restaurant.

"Thank you. Everything is excellent," he praised her and the other ladies.

"You don't know how much that means coming from someone like you. You're a five star chef with two highly successful restaurants. I know you wouldn't be giving this place praise if you didn't mean it."

"Sure, you're right," he replied.

"I, uh, see you were talking to Eva."

"Yes. I was. Although we didn't get a chance to talk like I had hoped."

"Do you mind if I share some things with you?"

Quentin looked at Avery with curiosity. "Sure."

"You see, uh, Eva—"

Ω

Everything was suddenly clear. It all made sense now that Avery had filled him in on what had been going on with Eva. He understood Eva's distance toward him, and it disturbed him. How could someone treat another person the way Harper treated Eva? As bad is it was to hear about Harper and Eva, and what she'd been secretly going through, this was his opening. He wondered if his grandmother knew the kind of man Dr. Harper Stenberg was. She'd told him time and time again the man was powerful and loved being in control, but to learn he was abusive and Eva was divorcing him was something he would never have imagined. There is no way she could know that side of Harper or she wouldn't have him in her circle regardless of him saving her life all those years ago. His grandmother was the epitome of grace and elegance and all things good. She surrounded herself with likeminded people, good people, kind people, generous people, and people of integrity. Quentin had learned Harper fit none of those categories.

Quentin was more determined than ever to remain in Eva's life. He wanted Eva Stenberg. No way could he just up and let her walk away. She'd never said she had feelings for him. Why would she when she was a married woman? But he was no fool; he felt the attraction between them, but because she was married, he restrained those feelings. Now it was no holds barred. He could see himself easy falling in love with Eva, and no matter how she fought against him, he was more encouraged than ever to make her his.

33

"All progress takes place outside the comfort zone." Michael Bobak

"The grand opening was spectacular wasn't it?" Avery beamed.

"It sure was," each lady agreed.

"It was just as good as the private opening, if not better," said Eva.

"Now on to the real business of running a restaurant. You ready, Eva?"

"Yep. How could I not be? This is a dream come true. Thanks to you all." She smiled big. Her life was changing for the better right in front of her eyes. She hadn't seen or heard from Harper and that was fine by her. If he had anything to say he talked through their lawyers.

The ladies sat in their new restaurant eating one of Eva's signature Bolivian dishes.

"Girl, this food is divine. I can't get enough," said Peyton.

"That means a lot, a whole lot coming from you, Peyton."

"How is the expectant mother feeling?" Meesha asked.

"Good, really good. I'm still in a state of disbelief, but I'm so grateful to God. I feel amazing!" Peyton rubbed her belly.

"Good for you, but let's revisit that when you start having morning, sickness," Avery said and chuckled.

"I know that's right," Meesha added.

"I've already started, believe it or not."

"Oh, my, that's quick," said Avery.

"That's what I thought," Peyton said, still holding her belly.

"Meesha, what about you and Carlton?"

"He had the nerve to show up at the house a couple days after we had the grand opening. Of course he couldn't get in, but one of the boys answered the door and let him inside."

"You didn't tell us," said Eva.

"I know, but I knew we were going to have ladies day out today so I planned to tell you all today."

"How did you handle that?"

"He called himself coming to get some more of his clothes and other personal items. When he found out there was nothing of his left you know he went clean off. The boys got upset because they'd never seen their father behave the way he was behaving. The man was ranting, raving and cussing like a sailor. Makena started crying and the boys, can you believe it, they started pounding on their father telling him to stop talking to me like that."

"That's those boys for ya," said Avery. "I heard boys go all out to protect Mommy."

"They sure did. Anyway, I told him he had to leave or I was going to call the police. Then he started crying and begging me to forgive him, talking about how sorry he was. Y'all, I told him yep you sure are sorry, Carlton Porter. Sorry you got caught. I walked to the door, opened it, and stood there. He got the hint and still crying like Makena, he left."

The ladies laughed.

"I feel sorta sorry for him," said Eva.

The ladies all focused on Eva.

"I don't know why you feel sorry for him," Meesha said, picking up a roll and taking a bite out of it. "Ummm, this is so good."

"Because he's lost such a beautiful family. What a shame."

Meesha's face softened and tears formed in the crest of her eyes. "Yeah, he did. I always thought Carlton and I would be together forever. You know?"

The ladies nodded. Avery reached over and touched her on the shoulder. "I know and I'm sorry."

"Me too," said Eva.

"Obviously, he didn't think about that when he was banging his sister-in-law," Peyton said.

"You're right. And Martin. Poor Martin. He's devastated. He put Evelyn out and he has the kids. He's filed for divorce too."

"Yeah, you told us. Good for him, but there goes another black family torn apart."

"Okay, enough of that. Eva, have you decided to give Quentin a shot?"

Eva blushed.

"Oooo, look at her, y'all." Meesha laughed and the other ladies joined in.

"I don't know. It's too soon but I have accepted his calls. But I'm still a married woman and I've been through too much with Harper to fully trust my heart to another. Quentin is a nice man. But I thought the same about Harper and look where it got me." A shroud of sadness came over her face.

"Give it time. One day at a time," Avery suggested.

"Pray about it," said Meesha. "God will give you the strength and he'll give you the answers you seek."

"Girl, forget Harper and give that man a shot," said Peyton and took a huge forkful of her cuisine and put it inside her mouth.

The ladies laughed again. Their friendship was solid although their individual lives had seen turmoil and some of life's most challenging times. Yet, the bond of friendship had supported each of them and given them a lifeline of hope to persevere and make it to the next hurdle of life.

34

"It's a difficult thing, but there are times when moving on with your life starts with a goodbye."
Unknown

One and a half years later...

"Harper, I'm ashamed to say this but what I've heard about you has been quite disturbing. You saved my life and for that I will forever be grateful, but your personal life leaves much to be desired and questioned."

"I don't know what you're talking about, Emma," Harper said, sitting across from the distinguished Emma Winters at the Beach Club.

"Your marriage or should I say lack thereof. How could you raise your hand against a woman? When I learned that you were abusing that poor, sweet wife of yours, I was appalled." Emma laid a hand against her thin chest frame, shook her head in disgust, and then took a forkful of her salad and placed it inside her petite mouth.

At those words the blood appeared to immediately drain from Harper's face and he looked whiter than a ghost.

"I...I don't know who told you that but I can tell you now, it's a lie."

Finishing chewing and swallowing her food, Emma picked up her cloth napkin, dabbled around her mouth and then proceeded talking.

"You should know that I don't repeat gossip, Harper, so don't you dare sit across this table from me and dispute what I've said. I have my sources, reliable sources at that and you're lucky you still have your position at Adverse City General. The best thing for you to do is give that girl whatever she wants in the divorce and then some. It's only a fraction of what you can do to make up for what you've done to her."

Harper sat quietly this time. There was nothing more he could say. Emma Winters was far too powerful of a woman to go against. She could end everything he'd worked hard for with just a few phone calls. It was bad enough that news of his impending divorce had been flashed across social media outlets and television.

"Do I make myself clear?" Emma said after reprimanding Harper as their lunch meal came to an end.

"Yes, of course. You've made yourself quite clear."

Harper walked Emma out to her waiting private car and watched as her driver opened the back door of the limo to allow her inside before he signaled the valet to pull his car around.

"God, I need you," he said as he got inside his car and exited the Beach Club. "I'm sorry for sleeping with the enemy. But don't forsake me, Father," he prayed as he continued driving toward Adverse City General.

The barrage of bad news didn't stop for Harper. Minutes of walking into his office at the hospital his cell phone rang.

"We're sorry to have to tell you this, Dr. Stenberg, but we think it's best to put your television show on hiatus until things simmer down," the executive producer said. "There's been too much publicity surrounding your personal life. Ratings have dropped tremendously. We'll be in touch," the man on the other end of the phone explained to Harper before ending the call.

Harper, sitting in his office at Adverse City General Hospital, gritted his teeth as he slammed his phone against the desk, cracking the screen. His life, his whole career, seemed to be melting in front of his eyes. His anger was fueled by all Eva had cost him. She had brought nothing but problems into his life ever since he met her. Filling for divorce was the ultimate betrayal besides her sleeping with his son. Not only had he lost his television show, she'd managed to turn his friends against him, particularly Emma Winters who had always been his staunchest supporter.

Tears streamed from his eyes as he rested his head into his hands. He didn't deserve this, didn't deserve any of this when he'd done nothing but provided for Eva and her parents. This was the payback he received? "God, don't you hear me?" he screamed and raised his fist toward the ceiling before breaking down and sobbing even louder.

Ω

The housewives made the decision to change the name of the restaurant to, *A Cut Above the Rest*. They agreed it was more in keeping with the elegance of the establishment and the type of food Eva offered. The former name, *Eva and Friends Bolivian Cuisine*, was too limiting because the restaurant offered more than Bolivian dishes. The name change didn't stop a thing because *A Cut Above the Rest* was definitely the talk of Miami and Adverse City. It was the go to place for fine dining. Celebrities dined there to the point it was a regular occurrence for paparazzi to be camped outside the restaurant waiting on the next famous face to enter.

True to her word, Emma Winters advertised the restaurant as the place to go, and it worked. Eva had appeared on television and in commercials and the restaurant had a strong social media presence too. With Quentin's help as well, her menu also expanded and according to food critics and customers her food was said to be some of the best in Florida.

The other housewives had taken a backseat to running the restaurant, allowing Eva to be executive chef and operating manager. Her parents were doing well, better than ever. She was grateful she had friends like Peyton, Avery, and Meesha who invested in the restaurant and provided financial assistance to her parents without expecting or asking for anything in return.

The way things were progressing in her life, soon Eva would be able to provide for her family on her own. Everything was finally falling into place—a really good place. She was still going through the divorce, but she was well provided for in alimony. A huge settlement agreement her lawyer told her would be coming from Harper in just a matter of months would make Eva a millionaire in her own right. Having never worked, other than the short stint she did for Quentin, Harper had been her sole supporter. For that he had to pay her dearly. She was able to keep the house but Eva told her lawyer she wanted to sell it instead. She was awarded two of their luxury vehicles, which she accepted. Other than that, she wanted nothing that would remind her of the life she lived with Harper, especially during the last horrific years of their union. She was now living closer to her restaurant in Miami and of course she brought along Marissa who Harper had tried to have deported. Thank God that hadn't worked out and Marissa was now studying to become a United States citizen and legal immigrant. It was still a process in the works but with the help of the housewives, Eva's lawyer, and the Winters' family of power, Marissa was going to be just fine.

"So, how are you enjoying running your own restaurant?" Quentin asked as they enjoyed lunch together.

"I'm loving it. I can do this forever, Quentin. And thanks to you, I've learned so much about the restaurant industry."

"I'm glad I could be of help. I've told you, Eva, I'm here for you. Whatever you need, all you have to do is call." He smiled a wanting smile. The more he was around Eva, the more of his heart she captured. He wanted her so badly, wanted to make love to her, to have her as his woman. He wanted to do any and everything to make her happy, if only she'd give him the chance. So far, all they shared were phone conversations, texts, and an occasional lunch.

Today was no different. He stopped in at *A Cut Above the Rest* on the pretense of wanting to dine at her establishment. It wasn't exactly a lie but the real reason he'd come was to lay eyes on her beautiful face. Her menu items were excellent but food was nowhere on his mind. His thoughts were constantly filled with the desire to be with Eva.

"I'm glad you stopped by," she said as she sat across from him in a private area of the restaurant.

"So am I," Quentin flirted. "Ummm, look, I don't mean to get into your personal affairs, but grandmother tells me your divorce should be settled in the new few months. Is that true?"

Eva looked up at Harper and paused eating. "Yes, unless he tries to throw a monkey wrench, as you Americans say, into things."

"I don't think he's going to cause you any more trouble or heartache. You shouldn't underestimate the power and influence of my grandmother. She tends to get things done rather quickly."

"I'm finding that out and I'm glad about one thing."

"What is that?"

"I'm grateful your grandmother is in my corner. Ever since the opening night of the restaurant when she saw Harper wasn't there, she reached out to me. At first I shied away from her, you know, I was just nervous. I didn't know who I could trust, but then the other housewives assured me Emma Winters was no fake person and if she was on your side you could expect her full loyalty. She's helped me in so many ways. It's like she's a grandmother figure to me. I didn't mean to confide in her the way I did, but she made it so easy to talk to her. I've grown to love her."

"My grandmother tends to have that effect. And you're right, if you have Emma Winters on your side, you have less to worry about. You deserve all good things in your life, Eva. God, how I wish you'd give me just a tiny piece of your heart. I promise I wouldn't hurt you, Eva."

Quentin stared deeply into Eva's eyes, reached across the table for her hand, but Eva pulled her hand back.

She looked around the restaurant. "I'm still legally married, Quentin. It's bad enough I'm sitting here having lunch with another man, but for that man to be you, well, I don't want Harper to have anything to use against me. You've never been on his favorite list of people, you know. Plus, I've been through too much with him already. I never know who he might have watching me."

Quentin scanned the private room where they sat. "Eva, look around. There's no one in here but the two of us."

"I know, but still. Please, just try to understand."

"I am trying, but it's hard for me to be around you and not be able to, well, to..."

Eva's heart raced. She didn't want to admit to Quentin yet her feelings. She wanted him just as much as he said he wanted her. She needed to be held, to be kissed, and to be loved, and she wanted Quentin to be all of the above. Yet, now was not the time. She had to do things right. Even Emma Winters has told her to do the same, to wait.

"After the divorce is final, you're free to do what you want, dear," Emma told her one afternoon when Eva visited the matriarch at her lavish mansion. "Maybe you and that grandson of mine can see where things lead. God knows he has it bad for you," Emma chuckled.

"Look, you said it yourself. My divorce will be final in a few months. If you can wait, then I want to see where things can lead for us. I like you a lot, Quentin. I *really really* do," she confessed.

"God, you don't know how much that means to me to hear you say that." He stood to his feet, walked around to where she sat, and guided her to stand by taking hold of her hand.

"I promise I won't rush you. I'll wait for you, Eva because I love you."

"You what?"

"You heard me. I'm in love with you, Eva."

"I...I don't know what to say."

"You don't have to say a thing. I see the answer in your eyes. Please, just this one time," he whispered, and gently pulled her into his arms. His kiss was deep, long, and full of passion.

Eva couldn't resist his touch, his fiery lips over hers, his hands as they familiarized themselves with her soft, shapely body.

Their moans were soft but intense as he continued kissing her until she eased out of his arms.

"Until the divorce," he said, and kissed her on the tip of her nose while he rubbed her long black hair.

She nodded and remained silent as they stared into each other's eyes. *I love you too, Quentin Winters. More than you'll ever know.*

35

"You can keep as quiet as you like, but one of these days somebody is going to find you." Haruki Murakami

Avery's life was going better than it had in years. She could honestly say she was happy and content being who she was. She was happy in her marriage, happy being a mom, and happy volunteering at Perfecting Your Faith Academy.

She and Ryker spent time traveling with and without the kids, something Avery always dreamed of doing. If she could have described it, she would say life was perfect. Her relationship with God was stronger and thanks to Meesha, she had found a sense of belonging now that she was working at the academy. It had given her a new type of freedom. Her baby boy was growing so fast. As a two year old, he was rambunctious and full of energy. Getting away from the house for a few hours every day was good for her. She felt it made her a better mother and wife all around.

"Girl, look," Avery said when the headlines on the television caught her eye just as she was about to exit Meesha's office. She stopped, turned around, and walked over to where the TV was mounted on the wall. Below it, the remote rested on a small table. Avery picked it up and turned the television up as their eyes remained glued on the reporter.

"What is it?" Meesha looked up momentarily from the computer screen. Her eyes widened when she saw the picture of Carlton and Perfecting Your Faith Ministries.

"After scandal and mayhem at Perfecting Your Faith Ministries, a church boasting over 20,000 members on the church rolls, Senior Pastor Carlton Porter was voted out by an overwhelming majority."

"His philandering ways finally caught up with him," a woman who said she was a member of Perfecting Your Faith told the reporter.

"You can't expect to do wrong and not be caught," a man said when the reporter approached him and asked for his thoughts about the Pastor's ouster. "I don't care what position you hold. God is going to bring your mess into the light."

"Thank you, sir," said the reporter. "Pastor Porter and Perfecting Your Faith Ministries is well known and highly regarded throughout Adverse City and beyond. Known for his philanthropic works and making an impact on the community with various ministries that extended all over Adverse City and throughout Miami and other neighboring cities, the church has taken a huge blow following Pastor Carlton's sudden forced exit. We don't have all of the complete details but what we do know is Pastor Porter has been accused of committing adultery with his brother's wife and a number of other women in the church. He is going through a divorce from his wife of over twenty years. They have six children. Who will lead this megachurch now? We've been told one of the associate pastors will fill in until a decision has been made about his successor. Stay tuned for more about this story as it unfolds. Reporting live from outside Perfecting Your Faith Ministries, I'm Neil Perry, News Channel thirty-four."

36

"You raze the old to raise the new."
Justina Chen

Peyton and Derek played with their eight month old twins, Liza and Lincoln, in their family room. The little girl and boy brought unspeakable joy to their lives. Liam was the perfect big brother and joined in on spoiling his siblings.

Peyton was a great mother, not that she hadn't done her best in raising Liam, but this time was different. She felt she had been given a second chance by God to raise her two bundles of joy in a sober state of mind.

Her marriage was stronger than ever and she wasn't going to do anything to jeopardize it ever again.

"Who would have thought we would be parents to twins," laughed Peyton.

"I know, right," said Derek. "When the doctor told us you were expecting twins, I thought I would pass out right there in the exam room." Derek chuckled.

"You turned crimson," said Peyton as she played patty-cake with the little girl who

Peyton was often told was the spitting image of her.

Derek hugged her twin brother and then threw him affectionately up in the air. "I still can't believe it. God showed up and showed out."

He sat back down next to his wife, leaned in, and kissed her affectionately while they each held the babies. When he pulled away he said, "I love you, Peyton Hudson. I've always loved you and I always will."

"And I love you, Derek Hudson. Always have. Always will."

Ω

The housewives gathered on the back lawn at Peyton's house for Ladies Day Out. The weather couldn't have been more perfect with sunny skies, a gentle breeze, and a temperature hovering between seventy to seventy five degrees. Unlike the other times when they met and enjoyed their day out dining at exclusive restaurants, shopping, and hanging out, this time the kids accompanied Meesha and Avery. Of course, Peyton's twins were there.

Eva's two Yorkie puppies, gifts from Quentin, were being pampered and petted by the older kids.

"Eva, the food is delish, as usual," complimented Peyton as she and the other housewives sat around the table eating.

"Yes, it sure is," Avery agreed followed by Meesha.

The ladies looked out on the massive grounds and surveyed their blessings.

"We've been through a lot," Meesha said, "but God has sustained each one of us. Plus, we're so blessed. Look at our kids. They're healthy and relatively happy. It's been hard on the boys, but as I'm watching them now I see how much God has enriched our lives in spite of their father's shortcomings." She became a little teary-eyed and hurriedly wiped her eyes before a tear could escape.

"And I couldn't be happier myself," said Eva. "I still can't understand Harper's treatment toward me. And to know because of him I lost my child, is something I have a hard time dealing with, but I'm still standing. I've found it easier to pray for him, which is something I didn't think I would ever be able to do."

"You're a good woman, Eva," Peyton assured her. "I know I talk out of turn sometimes, and you all think I can be heartless but all I know is how to speak the truth and say what's on my mind. If I've ever hurt any of you, I want you to forgive me. These past few years have shown me so much. Who would have ever thought that I would have two beautiful little babies." She looked out on the grounds at the nanny tending to her twins and smiled with tears flooding her eyes. Unlike Meesha, she couldn't hold hers back and the tears flowed down her rosy cheeks. She wiped them with the back of her hand before picking up a napkin off the table and using it to wipe the remaining tears.

"We're just so happy for you and Derek, Peyton," said Avery. "You guys are doing so well. And don't worry about your mouth; I think I can vouch for each of us that we know you all too well. Your bark is worse than your bite. And to be honest, you usually speak the truth, and the truth can hurt sometimes."

Meesha nodded followed by Eva.

"Yep, you're right about that, Avery," said Meesha.

"Meesha, you're a strong woman too," said Avery. "I don't know how you could move past all the hurt and heartache Carlton has caused you, but you seem to be forging ahead like a true champ."

"That's because she is," said Eva.

"Yep, you're right about that," said Peyton. "Meesha, you've always been a woman of faith. I'm sorry Carlton messed up a good thang. You're a remarkable woman, a great mother, and the best First Lady I've ever known."

"Thank you, but I have to confess it hasn't been easy. I've spent many sleepless tear-filled nights asking God why me and wondering what I did for Carlton to betray me. When I think about Martin and how his life and family was destroyed, it makes me even sadder."

"Yeah, I feel you on that," said Avery. "But he got custody of the kids and Evelyn, well you said nobody knows where she ran off to."

"No, I sorta think she's still somewhere laying up with Carlton. I have no proof of that, and at this point I couldn't care less what he's doing or what she's doing. They have their own beds to lie in."

"See, that proves you're a strong woman," said Eva. "I don't know if I'll ever be as strong as you are in the face of adversity."

"You already are. You're a survivor. Look at how far you've come since you and Harper broke up. Look how you fought back and now you're going to have more than you ever imagined having in your life," said Avery.

"And Avery, I hope you don't overlook your strength either" said Meesha.

Avery looked at Meesha strangely. "Me?" she pointed at herself. "I don't know how you could ever attribute strength to me. I'm the one who tried to end my life a few years back, remember? I'm the one who's always falling apart at the slightest bit of turmoil in my life. I'm no way near strong."

"Oh, yes you are. You're stronger than you think," Meesha said.

"She's right, Avery," Peyton chimed in. "So you tried to kill yourself, but thank God He didn't let you succeed. But you've grown stronger since then. You've always been the voice of reason for all of us in your own way. You're a fantastic mother and human being."

"And there's nothing you won't do for your friends. I'm a witness to that," said Eva.

"Ladies, I've come to realize there are some things we'll never know or understand, but that's okay because God knows what He's doing. I'm going to continue to lean and depend on him. That's all I know how to do." Her little girl toddled around her feet as Eva's two pups came scurrying around her and causing the little girl to start giggling.

The ladies laughed as they watched her before Meesha's nanny came and got Makena and took her to the wading pool.

"Now you're not only the head honcho at Perfecting Your Faith Academy, you're on the board at the church and several of the other outside organizations once headed by Carlton. You're a woman in power. We're proud of you. You've always set the example for each of us to follow whether I admitted it or not," Peyton boldly stated.

Eva got up from her chair and went over and hugged Meesha. Afterwards, Meesha, Peyton, and Avery followed suit. The ladies embraced in a big group hug.

"Let's have a toast," suggested Peyton.

"Cool," they said collectively.

Each housewife picked up their glass from off the table, raised them in the air, looked out on the luscious, landscaped grounds, and then turned and looked at each other, before clicking their glasses together and saying, "To the Real Housewives of Adverse City."

Words from the Author

Here we go again, delving into the lives of the rich and fabulous housewives of Adverse City. These ladies may be wealthy but are they so different than those of us with a limited amount of resources or money? I don't think they are. I've said it before, money and power does not and cannot erase what the true essence of a person is on the inside.

Wealth and power cannot erase feelings of guilt or self-condemnation over the mistakes we make. It cannot give us a clear conscious or assure we have the best of health. It cannot always alleviate worry and stress over the blows life often dispenses.

Of course, I can't deny wealth can help in many ways but can it help in the ways that really count in this life? Those things that come from having a good spirit? Can it give a person integrity and good character? Can it make us good people, nice people, compassionate people, empathetic people, loving and kind people? If these things are not already embedded in us, then I think not.

Next, I want to say to any and every one, male or female, boy or girl, accepting abuse whether verbally, emotionally or physically at the hands of another human being is **never** okay. Belittling others is **never** okay. I don't care how much money and power you possess, it is not right to treat another person in such a manner.

Lastly, be the kind of person who stands up for what is right. Seek forgiveness when you wrong someone—and that also means forgiving yourself.

Let's hope these housewives continue to evolve for the better in their lives, relationships, careers and family. May each of you do the same.

Shelia E. Bell
God's Amazing Girl

Contact information
www.sheliaebell.net
www.sheliawritesbooks.com
sheliawritesbooks@yahoo.com
www.facebook.com/sheliawritesbooks
@sheliaebell (Twitter & Instagram)
@literacyrocks (Instagram)

Follow me on Amazon bit.ly/sheliabell

Please join my mailing list for literary updates
and new book release information
www.sheliawritesbooks.com

If you enjoyed this book please go to your
favorite review site and leave a positive review!

Follow my Amazon Author Page bit.ly/sheliabell

Other links to my books

bit.ly/sheliaebell
bit.ly/sheliabn

www.ingramcontent.com/pod-product-compliance
Lightning Source LLC
Chambersburg PA
CBHW020416260626
47156CB00007B/2420